THE BARBARA CARTLAND ETERNAL COLLECTION

The Barbara Cartland Eternal Collection is the unique opportunity to collect all five hundred of the timeless beautiful romantic novels written by the world's most celebrated and enduring romantic author.

Named the Eternal Collection because Barbara's inspiring stories of pure love, just the same as love itself, the books will be published on the internet at the rate of four titles per month until all five hundred are available.

The Eternal Collection, classic pure romance available worldwide for all time .

I0620759

THE GOLDEN ILLUSION

Barbara Cartland

Barbara Cartland Ebooks Ltd

This edition © 2018

ISBNs

9781788671477   EPUB

9781788671484   PAPERBACK

Book design by M-Y Books
m-ybooks.co.uk

THE LATE DAME BARBARA CARTLAND

Barbara Cartland, who sadly died in May 2000 at the grand age of ninety eight, remains one of the world's most famous romantic novelists. With worldwide sales of over one billion, her outstanding 723 books have been translated into thirty six different languages, to be enjoyed by readers of romance globally.

Writing her first book 'Jigsaw' at the age of 21, Barbara became an immediate bestseller. Building upon this initial success, she wrote continuously throughout her life, producing bestsellers for an astonishing 76 years. In addition to Barbara Cartland's legion of fans in the UK and across Europe, her books have always been immensely popular in the USA. In 1976 she achieved the unprecedented feat of having books at numbers 1 & 2 in the prestigious B. Dalton Bookseller bestsellers list.

Although she is often referred to as the 'Queen of Romance', Barbara Cartland also wrote several historical biographies, six autobiographies and numerous theatrical plays as well as books on life, love, health and cookery. Becoming one of Britain's most popular media personalities and dressed in her trademark pink, Barbara spoke on radio and television about social and political issues, as well as making many public appearances.

In 1991 she became a Dame of the Order of the British Empire for her contribution to literature and her work for humanitarian and charitable causes.

Known for her glamour, style, and vitality Barbara Cartland became a legend in her own lifetime. Best remembered for her wonderful romantic novels and loved by millions of readers worldwide, her books remain treasured for their heroic heroes, plucky heroines and traditional values. But above all, it was Barbara Cartland's overriding belief in the positive power of love to help, heal and improve the quality of life for everyone that made her truly unique.

AUTHOR'S NOTE

The history of Blanche d'Antigny and Marguerite Bellanger is authentic. Blanche inspired both the novel *Nana* by Zola and the picture of *Nana* by Edouard Manet. She was the prototype of a *cocotte*.

Her lovers were incalculable because she was warmhearted and generous and could never say 'no' to any man who wanted her. Maharajas, Khedives and Shahs frequented her on their visits to Paris and Princes, Noblemen, bankers, actors and paupers beat their way to her *Salon des Amoureux*.

She not only appeared on the stage in Paris but also in London where she fell in love for the first and only time with an actor. When he died of consumption she borrowed the money for his funeral because she explained,

"I don't want him to be buried with the money I've earned in bed."

She died of smallpox when she was thirty-four.

Marguerite Bellanger attended Napoleon III's funeral when he died in exile in England. Like many *cocottes* she longed for respectability and was well known for her charity work.

In 1886 walking in the grounds of her Château, given to her by one of her lovers, she caught a chill, which developed into acute peritonitis.

A jealous old servant turned away the village *Curé* who wanted to administer the last rites to her and slammed the door in the face of her family.

Marguerite died alone in her forty-sixth year.

CHAPTER ONE
1869

The Marquis of Darleston took a sip of champagne.

As he did so, he told himself that there was really no need for champagne since the sea was calm and he seldom drank during the daytime unless there was a necessity for it.

Seated in his First Class cabin aboard the Steamship that carried passengers between Dover and Calais, his eye fell on his despatch box and he thought that he might well pass the time in reading some of the memoranda that the Prime Minister had given him.

But just as his hand went out towards it, the door of the cabin opened and to his surprise a woman came rushing in.

The Marquis was about to tell her that the cabin was private and that she had made a mistake when he saw her face and realised that she was frightened and obviously very young.

With his first look at her, the Marquis also realised she was extremely pretty.

"I am – sorry," she stammered in a soft breathless voice, "b-but could I p-please stay here for a moment?"

She looked over her shoulder as she spoke, as if to make certain that the cabin door was firmly closed and then she added,

"There is a man – he will not – leave me alone."

The Marquis rose to his feet.

"Come and sit down," he suggested. "I will deal with anyone who is making himself unpleasant."

He would have moved towards the door, but the young woman's hand went out as if to stop him.

"No – no, please," she said. "I don't want any trouble. It was – my fault for going up on deck, but people were being sick down below even though it is so calm."

The Marquis indicated a chair.

"Sit down. I will give you a glass of champagne. You will feel better after it."

She made no protest and he poured some of the champagne from the bottle cooling in an ice-bucket into a glass that stood on the tray beside it.

He turned to hand the glass to the woman and saw that he had not been mistaken in his first impression of her. She was lovely, in fact quite unusually so.

At the same time he could see that she was plainly and quietly dressed.

"Surely you are not travelling alone?" he asked. "Someone is with you?"

"There was – no one who could accompany me," she answered in a low voice.

She took the glass from him and looked at it doubtfully.

"I have – never drunk champagne before," she said after a moment, "but Mama often spoke about it."

She felt as if the Marquis was waiting for an explanation and then added,

"My mother was French."

"I think perhaps we should introduce ourselves," he said with a smile, re-seating himself on another chair. "I am the Marquis of Darleston."

"My name is Linetta Falaise."

"I am delighted to make your acquaintance, Mademoiselle Falaise," the Marquis said with a smile that most women found irresistible.

Linetta made a little inclination of her head that he thought was attractively graceful, but then he told himself that she had an unusual grace about her every movement.

Perhaps it was because she was so small-boned that in appearance she seemed little more than a child and there was something very young and untouched about the small oval face with its very large eyes and tiny straight nose.

She did not look French, the Marquis told himself, and yet there was definitely something un-English about her, despite her hair, which was very fair indeed.

Her eyes were unexpectedly the grey-blue of a stormy sea and perhaps it was her French ancestry that had given her her dark eyelashes in an almost startling contrast to her hair.

As if she was aware of what he was thinking, Linetta went on a little nervously,

"My mother came from Normandy, so she had fair hair unlike most Frenchwomen – and my father was also blond."

"You have been to France before?" the Marquis asked and it was more of a statement than a question.

Linetta shook her head,

"No," she answered.

"But now you are going to your relatives in Normandy?"

"I have no – relatives. I am going to a – friend in Paris."

"Then perhaps she is meeting you at Calais?"

Again Linetta shook her head.

"No, I must find my own way, but I am sure that everything will be – all right once I am there."

There was a doubt in her voice that the Marquis did not miss.

Then he told himself that it was none of his business. It would be a mistake to become embroiled in a stranger's affairs and he must concern himself only with the somewhat difficult task that awaited him once he reached Paris.

Equally he found that he could not help being curious about Linetta Falaise.

It was not only her attractions which were obvious enough, it was also it seemed to him, although he thought it absurd, there was something different about her from the average young woman he met in London and on his travels.

She had taken a few small sips of the champagne and now she said,

"Mama was right. She always claimed that champagne had an exciting taste about it that is quite different from other wines."

"You sound as if you are an expert," the Marquis smiled.

Linetta looked confused.

"I do not wish to sound presumptuous," she said, "it is just that Mama knew about wines and she taught me how to choose a good one, although we could seldom afford to drink anything but water."

She smiled at him as she spoke as if it was a joke and he told himself that it was ridiculous that she should be travelling alone.

It was quite obvious that she would be insulted by the attentions of strange men who would think that an unattached woman, especially one so pretty, was fair game.

"What made you come into this cabin?" he then asked her.

Linetta dropped her eyes and he thought that a faint flush relieved the pallor of her cheeks.

"I saw – you come aboard, my Lord," she replied, "and I thought how – distinguished you looked."

She hesitated and the blush deepened.

"I somehow – felt that I would be – safe with you."

"You are quite safe," the Marquis nodded gravely. "At the same time I think it is a great mistake for you to travel all the way to Paris without the protection of a chaperone."

"I know quite well it is – incorrect," Linetta answered, "but there was – nothing I could do – about it."

*

She had not been able to believe what she was hearing when Mademoiselle Antigny's tired voice had said a little above a whisper,

"I have been – thinking about you, Linetta. You will have to go to my – niece in Paris. There is – nowhere else. Nowhere!"

"Don't talk like that, *mademoiselle*," Linetta begged her. "You will get well – you must."

But even while she spoke with passionate intensity, she had known in her heart that there was no hope.

She had seen the doctor's face when he came from Mademoiselle's room the first time she had sent for him.

She had known then, even while he spared her feelings, that the Governess she had known and loved ever since she had been a child was dying.

"There is – something I have to tell you," Mademoiselle Antigny said with what Linetta knew was a tremendous effort.

"What is it?" she enquired. "But you must not tire yourself."

"I meant to tell you this a long time ago," Mademoiselle replied, "but I kept – putting it off, thinking there was no hurry. But now I have – not very long."

Linetta's fingers tightened on the old woman's hand as it lay on the sheets and she put her head forward so that Mademoiselle would not have to raise her voice and waited.

"After your mother – died two years ago," Mademoiselle began, "the money she lived on was – stopped."

"Stopped?" Linetta repeated in surprise.

"There was a letter saying that the allowance she had received every three months after your father died would no longer be – continued. You will find it in the – middle drawer of my desk."

This sentence had taken a great deal of Mademoiselle's strength and now she lay fighting for her breath and after a moment Linetta asked her,

"Then what money have we been spending?"

"My – savings."

"Oh, no, *mademoiselle*! How could you have been so generous, so kind? I should have found work. I should not have let you spend your own money on me."

"You would have had it anyway – when I was – dead," Mademoiselle replied. "But now, dearest, it has all – gone!"

She gasped for air again and then she said,

"When I am dead you must sell – everything and with the money you receive for the house and the furniture, you must go to – Paris. I cannot write to my niece, but you can write – the letter for me and I will – sign it."

"How do you know that she will want me?" Linetta asked.

"Marie-Ernestine is a kind girl. She will – look after you and find you – employment," Mademoiselle replied.

Then she choked and Linetta rose quickly to bring a tablet and a glass of water from the washstand.

These were tablets, which the doctor had prescribed to be taken only in an emergency, but she knew that, if Mademoiselle was to dictate the letter as she wished to do, this was in fact an emergency.

She supported the Governess's shoulders skilfully with one hand and having given her the tablet held the glass of water to her lips.

As she swallowed, Mademoiselle Antigny lay back for a moment or two against the pillows with her eyes closed.

Linetta went to the desk and brought back some writing paper and a pencil.

It would be better, she thought, if she took down what her Governess wished to say first as quickly as possible and then copy it out neatly.

After a few moments Mademoiselle Antigny's eyes opened and she said,

"As I was telling you – Linetta, Marie-Ernestine is a – kind girl. I helped to care for her until her – mother summoned her to – Paris."

She gave a little sigh.

"Poor Marie-Ernestine. She hid herself in the attic in despair – she could not bear the thought of – leaving the countryside. She wrote to me telling me about the Convent School where she was sent by a – friend of her mother's. Since then she has written to me every – Christmas."

"Yes, I remember how pleased you were to receive her letters," Linetta pointed out.

"Marie-Ernestine must have found good – employment in Paris," Mademoiselle Antigny went on. "She has not told me what it is – but her mother did sewing and housework for some distinguished families. Marie-Ernestine wrote this Christmas from a new address in the – *Avenue de Friedland.*"

Mademoiselle Antigny closed her eyes for a moment as if she realised that she was using up a great deal of her strength.

"Take down the letter – my dearest," she said and Linetta obeyed her.

The letter had been the only thing that gave her a feeling of protection after Mademoiselle had died and the house where she had lived with her mother ever since she could remember had been sold.

She knew that Mademoiselle had been wise in her suggestions. It was impossible for her to five alone.

In Paris, she told herself, Marie Ernestine would find her work of some sort and at least she would have one friend who she could turn to in trouble.

It seemed extraordinary, as she thought about it, that there were so few people in her life, which had centred entirely around her mother and her Governess.

They had been very isolated in the little village of Oakley where her mother had lived ever since she had married.

It was deep in the heart of the country. There was a stagecoach that passed through it twice a week, although no one seemed to get off and only very occasionally one of the villagers travelled on it into Oxford.

Her mother never seemed to wish to go to Oxford, Linetta remembered.

There was really nothing they needed and they had been content in the small house with its pretty garden, which Mrs. Falaise tended without a gardener.

'Perhaps it is because Mama is French that she knows so few English people,' Linetta would often tell herself as she grew older.

But she knew that the real reason was that her mother did not wish to meet strangers. She liked being alone, until, when Linetta was eleven, Mademoiselle Antigny, who had been teaching her, came to live with them.

It had been a successful arrangement because Mademoiselle after many years of teaching the children of Noblemen's families both in France and England, had retired to a tiny cottage in the village that had been provided for her by her last English employer.

When she had first begun to teach Linetta, sometimes her old pupils would call to see her.

They were elegant, sophisticated young women, now with husbands and babies, finding it amusing to talk over old times and to remind their ex-Governess how they tried to evade their French lessons.

But as the years went by they no longer came and Mademoiselle Antigny was thankful to have the companionship of Mrs. Falaise and the small comforts of the larger house that she had missed in her own cottage.

Her mother and Mademoiselle had always talked in French together, but they had both been insistent that, while Linetta's French should be perfect, her English should be equally good.

"Your father was English," her mother would say, "and he had such a beautiful voice. I used to tell him that when he talked it was like hearing music."

"Tell me about Papa," Linetta would sometimes reply when her mother made such remarks, but the moment she asked the question it would seem to her as if her memories were too painful for her mother to speak about them.

"He is dead, Linetta," she would say with a little sob in her voice.

Then slowly she would get up and go from the room as if she was afraid to lose her self-control in front of her daughter.

Linetta had looked round the house the night before she left for Paris.

'This has been my world,' she told herself, 'and I am leaving it all behind.'

The pieces of furniture that her mother had always loved and which had looked so elegant in the sitting room had gone.

They had fetched very little money and the bookshelves were empty and Linetta thought that more than anything else she would have liked to keep the books that had been her closest companions ever since she could read.

But they were too heavy to take to Paris with her and she felt somewhat guilty that she had so much luggage as it was.

Not that she had many clothes. There had never been much money to spend on what her mother with a smile called 'frills and fancies'.

But she had kept back from the sale many little objects that had been her mother's personal possessions and which she knew were the only mementoes left of her home and the life that she had lived as a child.

Last thing of all she had gone to the churchyard to her mother's grave. Mademoiselle Antigny, being a Catholic, had been buried elsewhere.

There was a headstone over her mother's grave, a very plain one. Linetta had not been able to afford anything elaborate, but it bore the name *Yvonne Léonide Falaise. Born 1832. Died 1867.*

'I wonder where Papa is buried,' Linetta thought to herself.

It was something that she had never asked her mother.

"Why do I use Mama's surname?" she had asked Mademoiselle when they were choosing the headstone.

"Your mother never told me," Mademoiselle answered, "but I believe it is because she loved your father so desperately that when he died she could not bear to talk about him or bear his name."

"Mama adored him," Linetta said softly,

"He must have been a very fine man to inspire such love," Mademoiselle remarked.

Of that Linetta was absolutely sure.

She laid on the grave the flowers that she had picked in the garden that morning. There were columbines, the herald of spring, primroses and a handful of snowdrops that had come out late this year.

Linetta had knelt down on the cold grass and prayed that Mademoiselle, like her mother, was in Heaven and that they would find each other.

Then she prayed for herself.

'Please, God, look after me and keep me from all harm. Help me to be good, to remember all the things that Mama taught me and help me not to be afraid.'

Mama and Mademoiselle would be looking after her she thought, wherever they might be. Their love for her would never die, just as hers for them was as warm and glowing in her heart as it had been when they were alive.

Nevertheless it had been difficult not to feel afraid when the moment had come to wait for the stagecoach that was to carry her on the long journey to Dover.

She had to change coaches more than once and she was always nervous in case her luggage was mislaid.

But somehow, mostly because people were kind to her and realised how inexperienced she was at travelling, she had reached Dover safely to find that she had only a little while to wait before the cross-channel Steamer left the Harbour.

She had never been in a Steamer before and she thought that it was large and very impressive.

Because a Steward directed her to do so, she went below and sat in the comfortable Saloon where there were other ladies, some with small children.

As soon as the Steamer started, the children became a nuisance and many of the other passengers began to be desperately sick.

There appeared to Linetta to be no reason for it as there was very little movement of the ship and she thought much of it must be because they were in a nervous state at having to travel at all.

Because she wanted some air and also to see a little more of the ship that she had gone up on deck.

A man had approached her wearing a plaid tweed cape and a hat of the same material.

He was, she knew by his voice, not a gentleman, but she had answered him politely because at first she had not realised that he was trying to be anything but helpful.

He pointed out the White Cliffs of Dover behind them, told her how long it would take them to reach Calais and informed her that this was no less than his twelfth visit to France.

She had moved away from him, but he became insistent that they should have a drink together.

"If I'd known I was going to meet someone as pretty as you on board," he said, "I'd have booked a private cabin. They're all engaged now, but we'll find ourselves a comfortable spot out of the wind."

There was something in the way he spoke that made Linetta feel apprehensive.

"I must go below," she insisted, only for him to reach out and catch hold of her wrist.

"You're going to stay with me, my pretty," he carried on. "We've got a lot to say to each other."

He put his arm round her as he spoke and his red face was unpleasantly close to hers.

Linetta fought herself free and ran along the deck. She heard his footsteps coming behind her and knew in a panic that she would not be able to escape from him for long.

It was then she remembered that, while she was waiting to go aboard, she had seen a tall distinguished man, accompanied by a valet and two porters carrying his luggage and coming from the Railway Station that adjoined the Port.

Linetta had in fact wanted to reach Dover herself by train, but it had been much more expensive than the old-fashioned coach, which had become little more than a carrier of goods for the last part of the journey.

She had looked with interest at the railway passengers as they walked towards the Steamer and it was obvious that there was no one more outstanding or indeed better looking than the traveller whom she had noticed immediately.

He was, she thought, quite different from any gentleman she had seen before.

She had, of course, seen quite a number in the distance during the years, the hunt had met occasionally in the village and besides the local Squires, some of whom she knew by sight, there had been the country Noblemen riding magnificent horseflesh and looking extremely autocratic in their pink coats and top hats.

The man walking from the train towards the ship had, in Linetta's eyes, been the embodiment of everything she thought of as handsome in a man.

'That is how my father must have looked,' she told herself.

Over the years, because her mother would tell her so little about her father, she had created in her mind a man who embodied in himself all the heroes of the books that she read so avidly.

Her father, she was sure, was like Richard Coeur de Lion, as Sir Walter Scott described him, like Jason in search of the Golden Fleece, David as Michelangelo had sculpted him and most of Shakespeare's heroes all rolled into one.

But she had never really been able to visualise his features or know in what way she resembled him.

Yet, when she had watched the gentleman she now knew was the Marquis of Darleston walking up the gangway of the *S.S. Victoria*, she told herself that that was how her father would have appeared when he was alive.

She set down her glass of champagne that she had taken only the minutest sips from and said now, almost like a child who has remembered its manners,

"I am very grateful to you, my Lord, for letting me stay here. You must think it very – forward of me to have come into your – cabin as I did, but I did not know what – else to do."

"I think you did exactly the right thing, *mademoiselle*," the Marquis said. "And, when we reach Calais, I will see that you are in a carriage that is reserved for ladies only."

"Thank you, my Lord," Linetta replied quickly. "I did not know that there were carriages like that."

"As I said before, you have no right to be travelling alone," he remarked. "But, of course, it is none of my business. I will just make sure that you are safe until your friends meet you in Paris."

Linetta opened her lips to say that she had no one to meet her, since Marie-Ernestine Antigny to whom she was carrying her aunt's letter, had no idea that she was coming.

Then she thought that it would seem as if she was asking the Marquis to give her further attention. And so she said nothing.

She would be able to hire a cab, which she knew was called a *voiture*, when she reached the *Gare du Nord*. She could give the driver Marie-Ernestine's address and after that everything would be all right.

She had a child's faith in what had been planned for her. It never occurred to her for a moment that Marie-Ernestine might be away or have changed her address in the two months since she had written to her aunt at Christmas.

"You are very kind," she said now to the Marquis and there was a look of trust in her face that he found touching.

Nevertheless when they reached Calais and he had personally found a carriage marked *Les Dames Seulement*, he had gone to the luxurious First Class compartment that had been engaged for him before he left England, telling himself that he had done his duty and nothing more could be expected of him.

While he was waiting for the train to start, he settled himself down intending to open his despatch box and make a start on the work that he had been unable to do while crossing the Channel.

When his valet brought a large hamper into the carriage, which he knew contained his dinner, it occurred to him that Linetta had not known that if she was to eat before she reached Paris she would have to buy food at the Station.

On an impulse which rather surprised him, he sent his valet to purchase at the buffet what he thought she would need and take it with a bottle of white wine to the compartment that he had found for her.

Then resolutely the Marquis had opened his despatch box and told himself that he had no wish for further interruptions.

Linetta was in fact surprised and delighted when the valet brought her the food and wine.

"His Lordship thought that you wouldn't have remembered, miss, that this be an Express and only stops once or twice durin' the night."

"Will you please thank his Lordship very much indeed," Linetta said. "I would have been very hungry by the time I reached Paris if he had not been so considerate."

"I'll tell him, miss."

Linetta wondered if she ought to tip the valet. He looked a very superior man and she was afraid that he would despise anything she could offer him.

Instead she added with a smile,

"Thank you too. I am very grateful."

"That's all right, miss," the valet said raising his hat.

To Linetta the Second Class compartment seemed very comfortable and she was fortunate in having only one other passenger with her, a middle-aged Frenchwoman who was travelling to Paris to join her husband, who had been transferred there from a Bank in London.

She shared Linetta's wine with her and gave her in return a cup of coffee that she had in a hay basket, which kept it warm for the whole of the journey.

She also showed her, as there was no one else in the carriage, how they could stretch themselves out comfortably on the seats and secure a little sleep.

Actually Linetta was so tired that she slept peacefully and did not wake when the train stopped at Amiens. She was only aroused when her travelling companion told her that they had only thiry minutes left before reaching Paris.

"Have you anyone meeting you?" she enquired.

"No, *madame*, I am going to find myself a *voiture*."

"Where are you going?"

"*L'Avenue de Friedland.*"

"Oh, that is indeed fortunate! My destination is in the same *quartier*. Let's share a *voiture*, it will be cheaper."

Under her friend's instructions, Linetta jumped out of the train as soon as it pulled into the Station.

The experienced Frenchwoman found a porter to carry their luggage and, because they had wasted no time and were ahead of the other passengers, managed to procure themselves a *voiture* immediately.

This meant, Linetta realised, that she would not have a chance of seeing the Marquis again to thank him for his kindness.

'I expect he has forgotten all about me by now,' she thought.

At the same time she knew that she would have liked to show her gratitude and, what was more, have another look at him.

It was very early in the morning and she had the feeling that the Marquis would not hurry as undoubtedly there would be a private carriage waiting to convey him to his destination.

'He is the best looking man I have ever seen,' Linetta told herself taking a last look back in case he would be standing on the platform.

"Come along," her friend urged her and she turned away knowing that she was quite ridiculously disappointed.

'I am sure that I shall never see anyone so handsome again,' she thought and knew that in future the heroes in the books she read would all look like him.

There was so much to see of Paris that it was easy to forget the Marquis as she sat forward on the edge of her seat to stare at the tall grey houses looking exactly as her mother had described them to her.

The cobbled roads that they were passing over were, she thought, very much as they had been in the past when the aristocrats had been forcibly taken to the guillotine.

Every stone in Paris, Linetta told herself, was redolent with history, a history that she had not only studied in her lessons but which she had also read with an eagerness that had made every word a joy in itself.

The Sun King, the intrigues of Statesmen such as Richelieu and Talleyrand, the rise and fall of Napoleon Bonaparte, she could never find enough books about them and now all she had read and all she had imagined she was seeing for herself.

It was only as she reached the *Avenue de Friedland* that she suddenly felt afraid.

Supposing after all that Marie-Ernestine Antigny would have nothing to do with her? How would she manage then?

Then she told herself that Marie-Ernestine would be just as her aunt had described her, a kind-hearted and friendly woman.

How could she be anything else when after all the years they had been apart she had still remembered her aunt at Christmas?

Mademoiselle Antigny had always read her niece's letters aloud to Linetta and she now wished that she had paid more attention to them.

They never seemed to say very much or even to describe Paris.

"I am very happy and doing well."

"I think of you so often, dear aunt."

"How I wish that my sister, Adelaide, was still alive and my little brother, Zacharie."

Linetta knew that Marie-Ernestine and her brother and sister had been the children of Jules Antigny, a carpenter who lived at Martizay near Bourges in the Indres.

She had also learnt that the carpenter had left his wife and family to run away with a local girl to Paris.

It was to search for him that his wife had entrusted her children to one aunt who lived at Mézières-Sur-Brenne and another who was fortunately employed as Governess at a nearby Château.

Having once reached Paris, she had found work for herself and sent for her eldest daughter. One of her employers, the Marquis de Gallifet, had later paid for Marie-Ernestine to go to the Convent des Oiseaux.

It had seemed, as Mademoiselle related it to Linetta, quite a lot to know about anyone, but now she felt that it was pitiably inadequate to tell her the sort of woman Marie-Ernestine had become.

She had worked it out before leaving England that Marie-Ernestine was twenty-nine and it was therefore eighteen years since she had seen her aunt.

'How could she really have known anything about her?' Linetta asked herself, as having said 'goodbye' to her friend from the train she found herself at the steps of number 11 *Avenue de Friedland* with her luggage beside her.

A moment after she had rung the bell Linetta wondered if in fact she should have gone to the door in the basement.

Perhaps the lady of the house would think it very strange for her to be calling on one of her staff and being so impertinent as to arrive at the front door.

But now it was too late for already she could hear footsteps and someone was drawing back the bolts of the door and then pulling it open.

It was a footman, but he was not wearing his liveried coat or his powdered wig.

Instead he was in his shirtsleeves, although he wore an ornate and colourful waistcoat festooned with gold buttons over his white shirt.

"I have – called to see – Mademoiselle Antigny," Linetta said nervously.

The footman looked at the luggage with surprise.

"She didn't say she was expectin' you."

"She was not aware of my coming," Linetta replied, "but I have a letter for her from her aunt."

"Mademoiselle d'Antigny's not awake yet," the footman said. "I suppose you'd better come in and wait."

He spoke doubtfully and Linetta looked at him in surprise.

It seemed rather a strange household where the employees did not rise until late in the morning and it had not escaped her notice that the footman had referred to Marie-Ernestine as 'd'Antigny'.

Only the aristocratic French prefaced their names with 'de' and Linetta felt that it must be a mistake.

She walked into a wall that was hung with tapestries and decorated with a number of exotic plants standing in large and very beautiful china bowls.

Crystal chandeliers hung from the ceiling and heavy blue velvet hangings were arranged over the mahogany doors.

The footman showed her into a small sitting room furnished to Linetta's astonishment in Oriental style. There were low red lacquered tables encrusted with silver and mother-of-pearl and on the tables there were gold boxes such as gentlemen used for tobacco and beside them cigarette holders.

Linetta's eyes were wide.

She had read about them, but she had never actually seen a cigarette holder, although she now recognised that was what they were.

Men out hunting smoked cigars, but cigarettes to her were something only to be found in fiction.

There was, however, a strong smell in the room, which Linetta knew was caused by people smoking there.

"If you'll wait here," the footman told her, "I'll find out from her maid when *m'mselle* is likely to be awake. I only hope I don't get into trouble for lettin' you in."

"I hope so too," Linetta said in a small voice.

It was bewildering to think that she was being treated like a guest of the lady of the house instead of a friend of one of the servants.

Perhaps, she thought, Marie-Ernestine had risen to a very important position over the years she had been working here.

Then she reminded herself that this was a comparatively new address.

It was all very puzzling and, as she looked around the room. she saw that it was unlike any room she had ever imagined could exist outside a book.

Then over the mantelpiece she saw that there was a picture.

It was a large painting of what Linetta thought must be intended to represent a Goddess. The woman, of Rubenesque proportions, was naked to the waist and the rest of her body was covered only with a blue cloth.

She was very lovely with large melting eyes, pink-and-white skin and softly parted red lips.

Linetta looked and saw that the frame had a plaque attached, on which was written, *The Repentant Magdalene* by Paul Baudry.

Linetta had seen many reproductions of famous pictures and twice Mademoiselle Antigny had taken her to London to the National Gallery because she and her mother both thought that it was part of her education.

Linetta was aware that this picture was well painted and wondered who Paul Baudry was. She had never heard of him as a great Master. But there was no doubt that he could paint and his model had been extremely lovely.

The door behind her opened.

"Madame says will you come upstairs?" the footman announced. "She'll see you."

Linetta's heart gave a little leap.

At least she had not been turned away from the door and she supposed that Marie-Ernestine was here. But who was Madame? Her employer?

"Thank – you," she managed to say quietly to the footman and followed him across the hall and up the stairs, noticing as she did so that he now wore his liveried coat.

They climbed to the first floor and the footman thrust open a door.

"The young lady to see you, *madame*," he said in what appeared to Linetta to be stentorian tones.

She walked in and for a moment she was too bewildered to notice anything but the bed.

It seemed to fill the whole room. It was hung with turquoise satin and the four-poster under its enormous baldachin of blue silk lace-trimmed curtains looked like a Throne half-hidden under clouds.

White bearskins served as a carpet and there was a heavy fragrance not only from the flowers which stood in great vases round the room but also from the exotic scent of patchouli and ambergris.

Linetta stood indecisive.

Then in the centre of the bed under a Venetian lace cover and sheets trimmed with wide lace someone heaved herself up against the pillows, someone with golden hair falling over her shoulders with a white skin and curved red lips.

It was someone Linetta had seen before and whom she realised immediately was the model of the picture downstairs, entitled *The Repentant Magdalene*.

CHAPTER TWO

The vision of beauty in the bed sat up and asked in a gay lilting voice,

"Who are you?"

Linetta walked a little nearer.

"I am Linetta Falaise – and I have a letter from Mademoiselle Antigny for her niece, Marie-Ernestine."

"From Aunt Teresa?"

Linetta started. Could this really be Marie-Ernestine?

She drew the letter from her handbag and coming nearer to the fantastic blue and lace bed handed it to the woman lying in the middle of it.

She thought as she did so that she had been right in thinking that the model in the picture looked like a Goddess. The milk-white shoulders and beneath them the pink-tipped breasts that were very evident under the diaphanous nightgown had a voluptuousness that even in her innocence she was aware of.

"How is my aunt?"

The question made Linetta realise, as she had been staring at her in a bemused fashion, that she had bad news to impart

"I-I am – afraid," she said hesitatingly, "that your – aunt is – dead."

"Dead?" Marie-Ernestine almost screamed and she crossed herself, murmuring as she did so,

"May *le Bon Dieu* have mercy on her soul. May she rest in peace."

The gesture made Linetta feel as if some of her surprise as well as her apprehension disappeared.

She noticed for the first time that Marie-Ernestine wore round her neck a little gold crucifix attached to a gold chain.

It hung in the valley between her breasts and seemed somehow a strange contrast to the exotic luxury of the bedroom.

Marie-Ernestine tore open the envelope and drew out the letter.

"I am afraid I had to write the letter for, your aunt," Linetta explained, "but she signed it the day before she died."

"I cannot imagine her dead!" Marie-Ernestine exclaimed. "She was my only living relative and the only one who still called me by my real name."

She paused, looked at Linetta and said,

"In Paris I am known as 'Blanche'. It was the name the girls at the Convent gave me because my skin was so white and no one addresses me anymore as 'Marie-Ernestine'."

There did not seem to be anything that Linetta could say, so she waited until raising her eyes once again from the letter Blanche said,

"Sit down. I see my aunt has set me a problem where you are concerned."

"I would not wish to be – any trouble," Linetta murmured humbly.

She looked around for a chair, found one and noticed that on a console table not far from the bed there stood an ivory statuette of Christ.

Like the gold crucifix round Blanche's neck it gave Linetta a feeling of comfort, even while it was impossible to think of this beautiful woman with the head of a *Bacchante* as Mademoiselle's niece.

Blanche went on reading the letter and Linetta noticed that her complexion was flawless.

She could quite understand why she had been nicknamed 'Blanche' and her mouth was curved exactly as Paul Baudry had portrayed it in his picture.

She was not to know that a year later Charles Dinet was to write about her,

"Her sensational mouth was meant to sing or drain a glass of champagne, the wine of love."

Linetta only knew that, despite her surroundings, Blanche seemed more approachable and more human than when she had first entered the room.

When she came to the end of the letter, Blanche raised her head and Linetta saw that her brilliant blue eyes were swimming in tears.

"She loved me," she wailed to Linetta. "Aunt Teresa always loved me. How I wish I could have been with her when she died."

"It was very quick," Linetta told her comfortingly. "She did not suffer very much. Even now I can hardly believe she is dead."

"She wrote to me of how happy she was living with your mother and teaching you," Blanche said. "But I always imagined you as well off and rich. Is it really true that you have no money?"

"None!" Linetta answered. "In fact, although I was not aware of it, your aunt spent all her savings on me these last two years since my mother died."

"I cannot imagine that she could have saved very much," Blanche commented. "Still there must have been something."

"I am so ashamed that I was not aware of her generosity," Linetta replied. "I would have found work of some sort, but I am not certain what I could have done, not in the village where we were living at any rate."

Blanche looked at Linetta and smiled. It was the friendly spontaneous smile of one woman to another.

"We will find something," she said with comforting conviction.

She rang the bell and a lady's maid, wearing a very smart starched linen and lace apron, came hurrying into the room carrying coffee and rolls.

There was coffee for Linetta too and not until the maid had left the room did she ask tentatively,

"Is this your house?"

"*Mais oui,*" Blanche answered. "But I have been here only a short time. I have been living in Russia for nearly five years."

"In Russia?" Linetta exclaimed in astonishment.

She could not have been more surprised if Blanche had said that she had been to the moon.

"I forgot, of course, and Aunt Teresa would not have realised it," Blanche responded. "Any letters I wrote to her were sent to France in the Diplomatic Bag. The post in Russia is hopeless."

"What were you doing in Russia?" Linetta asked.

"I was staying with – a friend," Blanche answered.

There was a perceptible pause before the last two words and Linetta had the impression that she had been about to say something else.

"It was exciting. Wildly exciting!" she went on quickly. "I had a large house in the Grand Morskoi, a legion of servants, *monjiks* they were called, and my salon was the smartest, the most amusing and undoubtedly the gayest in the whole of St. Petersburg!"

She gave a little sigh.

"*Hélas!* The luxury, the parties and the men of Russia are indescribable."

She paused to add as if to herself,

"The elite of St. Petersburg would assemble round my Samovar at eleven o'clock at night to talk, to drink wine, to sing and to make love!"

She gave a low laugh.

"At five the next morning, the silent *monjiks* would collect the guests who were still snoring in the corners of the room and take them home."

Linetta listened to her wide-eyed. Then as if in answer to a question that was in her mind, although it had not passed her lips, Blanche said,

"And, of course, I was a triumph at the French theatre!"

"You are an actress?" Linetta asked and knew that this was what she had wanted to know ever since she had entered the house.

"*Tiens!* Do you mean to say I forgot to inform Aunt Teresa that I was on the stage?"

"If you did, she did not tell me," Linetta answered.

"*Mon Dieu*! I am so used to it myself that I suppose I omitted to mention it. It must have been in 1858, all of eleven years ago that I made my debut as the living statue of La Belle Hélène in d'Ennery's *Faust*."

She laughed.

"I had nothing to say, but what they called my 'plastic beauty' was an enormous success."

Linetta realised that she was not boasting, she was merely stating a fact.

"But, if I was a success in Paris, I was a sensation in St. Petersburg and I suppose that the applause and adulation went to my head."

She gave a little laugh.

"I made a fool of myself!"

There was something endearing in the frankness of her words.

"What did you do?" Linetta asked.

Blanche laughed.

"In wild defiance of protocol I decided to attend the gala performance that ended the Winter Season at the Opera and I made up my mind to wear a gown which I would outshine both the others actresses and the audience in."

She looked so lovely as she related her story that Linetta was ready to believe she would outshine everybody and everything.

"I found exactly what I wanted at my *couturier*," Blanche went on. "The gown was superb. It had come from Paris and I knew that there was nothing like it in the whole of Russia. But it had in fact been ordered by the Czarina."

Linetta listened wide-eyed.

"I was mad! Of course I was mad," Blanche related. "The *couturier* tried to stop me doing anything so provocative, but I thrust a bundle of notes into his hand and hurried from the shop with the gown."

"What happened?" Linetta enquired.

"That evening I wore it and the Czarina seated in her box looked at me with an anger that she could not hide."

She paused to finish dramatically,

"The next day Mezentseff, the Chief of the Secret Police, was commanded to expel me from Russia!"

"Oh, no!" Linetta cried. "But that was cruel and surely the gown could not have been that important?"

Blanche did not trouble to explain that it was not only the gown but a great many other things that had incensed not only the Czarina but also all the other women of Social standing in St. Petersburg.

Instead she shrugged her shoulders and continued,

"It did not matter. When I returned to Paris, everyone was pleased to see me, and I knew the best way I could take my revenge on Russia was to make myself a distinguished member of the stage in France."

To Linetta it was like listening to a Fairytale.

She had the feeling that Blanche was not talking to her personally, but because she was connected with her aunt she was relating her life story as if to a relation.

She wanted her to know, wanted her to be impressed and to realise as undoubtedly Mademoiselle would have been what a success she was!

"I took lessons in declamation," she told Linetta, "and Madame Marchel, the pianist at the *École Lyrique*, made me practise songs from the *Opéra Bouffe*."

She made a gesture with her hands.

"I cultivated drama critics and celebrated actors and deliberately procured an introduction to the Editor of the *Gazette des Étrangers*."

"How did that help?" Linetta queried.

She was trying to understand exactly what Blanche was telling her and trying to follow every word.

"Can you not comprehend?" Blanche asked. "Henri de Père, the Editor of *The Gazette*, began to arouse public interest in me. After all I had been away from Paris for nearly five years. I was afraid that the public, who are very fickle, would have forgotten me."

"What did he do?" Linetta enquired.

, "A week before my debut at the *Palais Royal*, *The Gazette* published no fewer than eight paragraphs about me and right through until October *The Gazette* sang my praises both on the stage and off."

"That was wonderful!" Linetta exclaimed.

"It was indeed," Blanche agreed, "and now I am appearing at the *Folies Dramatiques*."

"May I see you?" Linetta asked breathlessly.

"But of course! At the moment I am playing Frédégonde. It is a delightfully dramatic part, but an even better one begins next month. Then I shall be established and Russia will be sorry they lost me!"

"What is your new part to be?"

"I shall be Marguerite in *Le Petit Faust*."

She looked at the diamond-encrusted clock that stood by her bed and said,

"That reminds me, I must get up. There is a rehearsal this morning. You must come with me. It will give you an idea of the role I am to play."

"May I really do that?" Linetta asked.

"But, of course," Blanche replied. "And as you will be staying here with me, I must introduce you to Paris."

She looked at her as she spoke, as if for the first time.

"Take off that ugly bonnet," she ordered. "You are pretty, very pretty, but your clothes are terrible!"

"We had very little money to spend on them," Linetta said apologetically, "and, of course, we were living in the country."

She took off her bonnet as she spoke and Blanche climbed out of bed as she did so.

Linetta could not help feeling embarrassed when she saw how little she was wearing.

She had never seen a woman naked before, her mother and Mademoiselle had always been very modest in her presence.

But Blanche seemed to be quite unconcerned that her white skinned, full-breasted nakedness was only just veiled by her nightgown and she looked more than ever like one of Rubens's Goddesses.

She stood for a moment staring at Linetta and then she exclaimed,

"You are lovely, really lovely! That childlike face with such very fair hair has a charm all of its own."

She gave a little laugh.

"We are certainly a distinct contrast and that in itself will be amusing."

She rang the bell and, when her maid came hurrying in, she said,

"I will have my bath now. Have you filled it with Montebello?"

"I have, *madame*," the maid replied. "Two hundred bottles!"

Blanche saw Linetta's look of astonishment and said,

"I find a mineral water bath very reviving and refreshing and I expect you too would like a bath having spent all night on the train?"

She turned to the maid.

"Show mademoiselle to the bedroom at the back which is quiet. Unpack for her and help her into her prettiest gown. We are going to the theatre."

"Very good, *madame*,"

Linetta found herself ushered along a passageway, which led to a room that was luxurious, but not as fantastic as Blanche's bedroom.

Her boxes were brought in and, while the maid prepared her a bath in an adjoining bathroom, she unpacked some of her gowns and hung them up in the wardrobe.

They were all, she thought, plain and dull by what would be Blanche's standards.

Then she told herself sensibly that it was of little consequence. No one would look at her when that beautiful creature with her golden hair, vivid blue eyes and amazingly white skin was in sight.

Finally, when Linetta was ready, she only had a quarter of an hour to wait until Blanche appeared wearing a blue and white costume that was so sensationally designed that she might have stepped straight off the stage.

But Linetta could look at nothing but the diamonds she was wearing.

Never had she imagined that anyone could wear so much jewellery, especially in the daytime. It seemed to her that Blanche literally glittered and the earrings that hung to her shoulders looked almost too heavy to be comfortable.

"Come along," Blanche urged. "I must not be late even though they will wait for me. We don't want to spend the whole day at the theatre."

Outside the house there was an exceedingly elegant carriage, the seats of which were covered in the same blue as Blanche's costume.

Linetta thought that it must be a coincidence until Blanche explained,

"My carriages always match my *toilette*. My *couturier* often has to supply the same material to the coach makers when they cannot obtain it themselves."

They drove off and Linetta's eyes turned from her flamboyant hostess to gaze at Paris.

The sun was shining and the chestnut trees were coming into bloom and she thought that it all appeared even more entrancing than her mother or Mademoiselle had told her it would be.

She stared at the cafes. Where already the customers were seated round the marble-topped tables.

She saw the wide boulevards filled with magnificent and extremely smart carriages, phaetons and curricles, all drawn by superlative horses and she knew that the ones that were drawing the carriage that she was seated in were finer than any she had ever seen in her life before.

She noticed that as they drove along women waved and gentlemen raised their hats and Blanche acknowledged their greetings with a gesture of her right hand.

"You have a great many friends," Linetta observed.

"They are not friends," Blanche explained. "I am one of the sights of Paris!"

"You must be a very famous actress!" Linetta exclaimed, but Blanche did not reply.

They arrived at the *Folies Dramatiques* and, as they stepped down from the carriage, Linetta thought with a feeling of excitement that she was about to enter a theatre.

She had been inside one only twice before when Mademoiselle had taken her into Oxford to see three of Shakespeare's plays, one of which had been performed in the open air.

The other two had been acted in the local theatre and, although Mademoiselle had been somewhat disparaging about the performances, Linetta had been entranced.

Now she was to see what a French theatre was like, but, as they walked in, she was immediately conscious of a feeling of disappointment that was like a blow.

The auditorium that loomed in front of them was a dark yawning void, unlit and illuminated only by a light from the stage. There was an atmosphere of dust and dreariness that was certainly not what Linetta had expected.

In the general gloom it was hard even to see the stage boxes and the red velvet of the seats looked dark and dirty.

There were several people on the stage but, as they were lit only by what appeared to be a stable lamp nailed to a post, the actors seemed to be illuminated like phantoms with their shadows dancing behind them.

The rest of the stage resembled nothing so much as a demolition yard. There were ladders and frames, stage props that looked like piled up rubbish heaps and overhead there were several backdrops that hung at different heights in the air like flags at half-mast.

Blanche. However, stepped forward and there was a cry from a man who was standing in front of the orchestra pit, a pile of papers in his hand.

"Thank God you've come, Blanche!" he almost exploded. "If we don't begin to make some sense out of this chaos, we'll never open on the 28th!"

Blanche gave a little scream.

"The 28th?" she exclaimed. "I thought it was next month."

"The 28th of April," the man emphasised firmly, "and if you want to be a success you will have to start working! You didn't know a single line of your part yesterday."

"I don't suppose they will ever listen to anything I say," Blanche replied with an amused laugh.

"*Non*! They will be looking at your body," he said. "But I still want the authors to have a chance."

"Why?" Blanche asked pertly.

She turned towards a door that led to the back of the stage.

"I'll take off my hat and then I will be with you."

Linetta followed her.

There was hardly room in the narrow passageway for Blanche to move with her large bustle, which swept out behind her like a tidal wave of blue and white frills.

Linetta had never realised until she had seen Blanche that a gown could be so enormous and yet be so graceful.

She had never worn a bustle or a crinoline, which it had superseded and she wondered as she followed Blanche whether she would be able to buy a gown in Paris with a small bustle cheaply.

The passages at the back of the stage were dark and dirty and their heels made a tapping noise on the stone floors.

There was an unpleasant smell, Linetta noticed, which she reluctantly identified as dirt, the stink of gas and what she thought must be glue used in the scenery.

Blanche opened the door of what was obviously her dressing room and now there was an overwhelming fragrance that fought valiantly with the other smells.

It was a square room with a very low ceiling and draped entirely with light brown cloth and a curtain of the same cloth hung from a copper rod to make a separate compartment at the far end.

There were two large windows opening onto the courtyard of the theatre and a tall mirror stood opposite a dressing table of white marble, which was littered with an assortment of scent bottles and glass boxes of cosmetic oils, attar of roses and powders.

There was a washbasin, which was full of soapy water, and a number of ivory toilet utensils and small sponges.

Linetta could see clothes hanging on a long rail at one side of the room and there were two armchairs and a table where stood two empty bottles of champagne.

And everywhere in the room, on the washstand, the dressing table and side tables, there were flowers.

They certainly added to the fragrance of the room, although some of them, Linetta noticed were half-dead.

Blanche seemed to notice neither the untidiness nor the squalor.

She took off her jacket and hung it up on a rail with the other clothes, removed her hat, which perched on top of her golden head, and set it down on the dressing table. It was an ultra-fashionable little hat, trimmed with blue and white ostrich feathers.

But Blanche's hair was so golden and her face so animated that Linetta could not help thinking that she looked even more spectacular without the hat than with it.

Blanche gazed at herself in the mirror and gave her reflection a little smile, as if pleased with what she saw, before she turned to Linetta,

"We will waste no more time here than we can help. I have a luncheon engagement which I don't want to miss and this afternoon I will take you driving with me in the *Bois de Boulogne*."

"I do not wish to be any trouble," Linetta pointed out humbly.

"But first," Blanche went on as though she had not spoken, "I must find you something to wear. You cannot be seen with me looking as you do now."

"I am sorry," Linetta replied apologetically and then, quickly in case Blanche had misunderstood what she had said already, she added,

"I am afraid I cannot buy any clothes at the moment as I have very little money left. What is important is for me to find some work so that I can pay for myself."

"There's plenty of time for that," Blanche said, "and it will amuse me to dress you so that you will look really pretty."

She walked from the dressing room as she spoke and, although Linetta wanted to protest, it was difficult to do so as their feet clattered and echoed in the narrow passage.

Blanche went onto the stage and Linetta sat in the auditorium.

Nobody paid any attention to her and she watched wide-eyed while Blanche seemed to bring gaiety and laughter to the general gloom of the theatre.

She hurried through her part and, when she sang, although Linetta realised that she had very little voice, she somehow made the whole thing amusing and gay so that the other actors and actresses seemed to come alive and even the harassed Producer appeared to be satisfied.

"Now I must go," Blanche said when they had been working for an hour and a half.

"But we haven't even touched the second Act," the Producer cried.

"My understudy can stand in for me," Blanche replied. "I have an important luncheon appointment."

She paused and, when the Producer would have gone on protesting, she said,

"I have to make sure that my gowns and my diamonds dazzle the critics."

Instantly the protest died away.

"We'll manage," he said quickly, "but you will come tomorrow?"

"I will do my best. If not, my understudy might well earn her keep now for, as you well know, I am seldom ill, so she never has a chance to play the part."

"That's true," the Producer nodded. "Your health, like everything else about you, is magnificent!"

He lifted her hand to his lips and kissed it, her hat and jacket were brought to her by an attendant and the Manager of the theatre, who saw Blanche to her carriage, also kissed her hand before they drove off.

"Well," Blanche quizzed Linetta, "what did you think of it?"

"I was disappointed in the theatre until you were on the stage," Linetta said truthfully. "It was so drab, so ugly, dirty and untidy."

Blanche laughed.

"Wait until you see me tonight as Frédégonde," she said. "Then everything will seem very different."

They drove on and after a moment Linetta asked,

"Are you lunching at home or are you going to drop me there?"

"We are going to have luncheon at *Aux Trois Frères Provençaux*," Blanche replied. "Your host will be Raphael Bischoffsheim and it is very important that he should like you."

"Why?" Linetta asked.

"Because he is a close friend of mine," Blanche answered, "and because I wish him to give you some very beautiful clothes, Linetta."

Linetta looked astonished.

"You mean – that he would – pay for my clothes?" she said in a voice hardly above a whisper. "B-but I could not – let him do that."

"It will not be a present to you but to me," Blanche said lightly. "Bisch always gives me everything I want. He is kind – very kind indeed!"

They drove on and after a moment Blanche added,

"We are lunching near the Bourse because that is where Bisch will be this morning."

Linetta knew that the Bourse was the equivalent of the London Stock Exchange.

"Is Mr. Bischoffsheim a Stockbroker?" she asked.

"He is a Banker," Blanche replied, "the richest and the most important one in Paris. He is also very generous, so make yourself pleasant to him!"

Her words made Linetta feel nervous. She was still worried in her own mind whether she should allow any man, whoever he might be, to pay for the clothes she wore.

She was certain that her mother would have thought it very improper, but she knew that it would be impossible for her to go about with Blanche wearing her drab unfashionable gowns that she had brought with her from England.

At the same time why should Mr. Bischoffsheim buy her gowns even if it was to please Blanche? It seemed an extraordinary idea to say the least of it.

It seemed even more extraordinary to Linetta when she met Mr. Bischoffsheim.

The restaurant was a small one, crowded with men, but there were a few women to be seen. Mr. Bischoffsheim, who was there before them, rose from his table in a corner where he already had the wine list in his hand.

He smiled as Blanche advanced towards him and kissed her hand.

Then he looked enquiringly at Linetta.

"This is a friend who arrived unexpectedly this morning," Blanche explained. "We have a lot to tell you."

Linetta curtseyed as another chair was brought to the table and Blanche seated herself saying,

"How are you, *mon brave*? Not too tired after last night?"

There was a caressing intimate note in her voice and it seemed to Linetta that she accentuated the words '*last night*'.

"You made me feel as usual very young and very ardent," Mr. Bischoffsheim replied.

He kissed her hand again and Blanche smiled at him beguilingly.

He was certainly not what Linetta had expected Blanche's friend to look like.

He was a thickset, heavily built man with a Roman nose. He wore the fashionable side whiskers and small imperial beard that was affected by a large number of Frenchmen because it was the fashion set by the Emperor.

Mr. Bischoffsheim was certainly not young, over forty at least, Linetta decided, but he was well dressed and wore a signet ring on his little finger in which there was a superlative ruby.

"Let's order before we do anything else," Mr. Bischoffsheim suggested. "I cannot stay long."

"You are busy?" Blanche enquired.

"Very busy," he replied. "The Bourse is up this morning after the gloom of last week." He then turned his attention to the menu discussing every dish in detail with the *Maître d'Hôtel*, who hovered at his side, and finally opening the *Carte des Vins*, considered what wines would go with the dishes he had ordered.

As if he realised that Linetta would have no preferences, he did not consult her, but ordered for her as he had already done for Blanche.

Linetta felt glad that she was not required to make any decision. Instead she looked around her and saw that many of the men present were looking at Blanche with unmistakable expressions of admiration in their eyes.

It was not surprising, Linetta thought, because, just as she had lit up the stage, she appeared like a light in the restaurant and her eyes seemed even more sparkling than the diamonds she wore on her bosom, in her ears and round her wrists..

"Now tell me about your new friend," Mr. Bischoffsheim enquired when finally the waiter had taken down their order.

Blanche explained to him about her Aunt Teresa and how, when she had died, she had sent Linetta to Paris.

"You have no relatives in England?" Mr. Bischoffsheim asked Linetta.

"None, *monsieur.*" she replied.

"What do you think she can do, Bisch?" Blanche enquired. "Do you think she would be a success on the stage? I am sure if I insisted they would find her a small part in *Le Petit Faust.*"

"Oh, no," Linetta said quickly. "I would be far too shy and besides I have no wish to work in the theatre."

As she spoke, she thought how drab and dingy it had appeared behind the scenes and of Blanche's untidy dressing room. She was quite sure that if the star of the show did not have better accommodation, those with only small parts would fare very badly indeed.

Mr. Bischoffsheim looked at Linetta with a speculative eye.

"I don't think that Mademoiselle Falaise appears to be particularly suited to a theatrical career," he said at last, "but there is no hurry. When she has been in Paris for a little while, she will doubtless find plenty of other occupations that will be more congenial."

"In the meantime she can stay with me?" Blanche asked. It was a question.

"But, of course," Mr. Bischoffsheim replied. "There is plenty of room."

"Then that is settled," Blanche said to Linetta with a little smile. "I told you Bisch would know what to do. You will stay with me until we find something that will interest you."

"I don't wish to be an encumbrance," Linetta stated, "and I thought it might be possible for me to find somewhere where I could teach English – perhaps in a school or in a private family."

Blanche gave a little cry.

"*Non, non!*" she exclaimed. "Can you imagine anything duller or more dreary than teaching other people's tiresome children? Besides what would you earn? Not enough to keep me in hairpins!"

Mr. Bischoffsheim laughed.

"It is not everyone, my dear Blanche, who expects them to be of twenty-two carat gold with diamond ends."

"You know what I mean. She is too pretty, Bisch, much too pretty to waste her time in a schoolroom,"

"I agree with you," Mr. Bischoffsheim replied, "and, as I have already said, there is no hurry. Take your time, *mademoiselle.*"

"Oh, do call her 'Linetta'," Blanche protested. "Mademoiselle sounds so formal. Besides she is my friend and you know I am never formal, am I, Bisch?"

"Sometimes regrettably informal," he answered.

"Now you are being horrid!" Blanche pouted. "I told you I was sorry."

"I hope you are really contrite and that it will not occur again," he declared and there was a note of seriousness in his voice.

Linetta felt a little *de trop* at this exchange, which made her realise that Blanche and Mr. Bischoffsheim must be very close friends indeed and she hoped he would not think that she was intruding.

It had not escaped her notice that Blanche had in effect asked his permission for her to stay in the house and she could not help wondering whether, as he was obviously so very generous with his money, that he had helped her to buy it.

Moreover she felt acutely embarrassed when Blanche put her hand on Mr. Bischoffsheim's arm and said,

"Please, Bisch, Linetta must have some clothes. I cannot take her with me in the *Bois de Boulogne* looking as she does now."

"No – please – " Linetta began to protest..

Blanche put up her hand to stop her from saying anything more.

"I have already told you that Bisch is the kindest, most generous man in the world, are you not, *mon cher ami*?"

"But, of course, I am," Mr. Bischoffsheim agreed. "Order what you like for little Linetta. It will not bankrupt me!"

"I should not allow any woman to do that except myself," Blanche smiled.

She slipped her hand into his.

"Thank you, Bisch."

He raised it to his lips.

"Have I ever refused you anything?"

"Nothing," she replied, "and I did see an entrancing necklace in Oscar Massin's."

"We will look at it together," Mr. Bischoffsheim said and kissed Blanche's hand again.

They left the restaurant by half-past two and by four o'clock Linetta owned what seemed to her to be an extravagant, overwhelming and stupendous wardrobe of new clothes.

Never had she imagined that she would ever possess any garments so attractive, so expensive and so very different from anything that she had ever owned before.

Blanche took her to Madame Laferrière in the *Rue Taitbout*, who dressed her not only on the stage but also off.

Madame Laferrière understood exactly what was required.

"Mademoiselle is so young, she has the look of a child."

"That is exactly what I thought," Blanche said, "and that, *madame*, is how she should be dressed."

"But, of course," Madame Laferrière agreed.

Materials were brought, lace, gauze, silks, tulle and, because it was fashionable, brilliant spangles, fringes that looked like golden rain and flowers that were so lifelike that Linetta could hardly believe they were artificial.

The latest gowns, she learnt, were very decorative. There were silks, puffs of tulle, draperies, ribbons and above all sprays of flowers. Lilies of the valley, roses, marguerites, orchids or anything that seemed to make each gown a fantasy world of the stage rather than for an ordinary Reception room.

But Linetta's gowns were in fact to be what Madame Laferrière considered to be very simple.

Snowdrops were to decorate one evening gown, a bonnet was to be trimmed with primroses and for another there were unopened rosebuds.

Finally Linetta was almost sewn into a gown that had been made for someone else, a bonnet was found to match it and. almost as if she was a magician, Madame Laferrière produced long gloves, a reticule and even little satin slippers that were very unlike the sensible shoes that Linetta had worn in the past.

Finally, when she was dressed, she hardly knew herself. She could not believe that this slim creature reflected in the mirror wearing a bustle of frills and bows beneath a tightly moulded bodice and a tiny hourglass waist could be herself.

And her face looked different too. The bonnet trimmed with rose buds and lace which might have been made by fairy fingers made her eyes seem even larger and more surprised than they were already.

"Everyone will want to know who you are," Blanche cooed as they drove back to the house. "I have just to change my *toilette* and then we will go to the *Bois de Boulogne*. I have ordered my *drojky* so that they will really pay attention to us."

Linetta did not really understand what she meant. She had ceased for the moment to grasp half the things that were happening to her. It was all too fantastic, too extraordinary and even now she could hardly credit that Blanche was really Mademoiselle's niece.

When Blanche changed into a sensational gown of scarlet fringed with white and with a small hat trimmed with white feathers perched on her golden hair, which cascaded down her back in curls, Linetta felt that it was all part of an act and the *drojky* was just a sensational prop.

"Do you know what I did before I left for Russia?" Blanche asked.

Linetta waited to hear.

"I drove in the *Bois de Boulogne* with a procession of thirty-seven carriages, each of them carrying one of my *toilettes*. Think of it! Thirty-seven *toilettes* and thirty-seven carriages in a row!"

Her voice was like a clarion call of triumph.

Linetta could believe anything and the *drojky* was like something out of a dream, carved and painted, the driver in scarlet silk blouse and white breeches was in charge of four wild Ukrainian horses.

Everyone turned their heads to look at Blanche and her companion from the moment they drove down the *Avenue de l'Impératrice* towards the *Bois de Boulogne*.

"We shall see everyone, *le tout Paris*, in the *Bois de Boulogne* this evening," Blanche told her with a note of satisfaction in her voice, "and there will be nobody, Linetta, nobody who will look more sensational than we do."

CHAPTER THREE

Linetta could not sleep.

She had thought when she went to bed that she felt so exhausted that it would be impossible to keep her eyes open any longer.

But once her head was on the pillow she found herself going over the fantastic unbelievable events of the day and re-living a panorama of excitement that made it impossible for her to sleep.

First of all in her mind there had been the drive in the *Bois de Boulogne*.

Even apart from Blanche and her sensational appearance in the *drojky* she had never imagined that so much which was elegant, colourful and luxurious could be gathered together under the trees that were green with the first buds of spring.

Crowds of exciting spectators were massed along the paths or the side of the roads to the *Grande Cascade*.

There were handsome smart men escorting women who were more extravagantly gowned than Linetta could have imagined in her wildest dreams.

Driving in *coupés*, Victorias, phaetons and four-wheeled carriages with a folding hood and in little wicker pony carriages beribboned with the colours of their own private stables, they made a poem of movement and brilliance combined with magnificent horseflesh.

There were also tandems, delicate as a piece of clockwork, eight-springed carriages fitted out in an aristocratic fashion to vie with the *calèches* drawn by *café au lait* coloured horses that belonged, Linetta learnt, to various fashionable ladies with whom Blanche was most closely acquainted.

They looked to Linetta like Birds of Paradise and, as Blanche chatted gaily about them, she grew more and more bewildered not only by their appearance but also by details of their private lives that she was regaled with.

"That is Cora Pearl," Blanche pointed out and Linetta saw a woman garbed in emerald green with a *calèche* upholstered in the same colour.

She was not pretty, in fact Linetta could not help thinking that she had rather a plain face, but according to Blanche she had very important friends.

"Cora is also one of the sights of Paris," Blanche explained. "Her *cher ami* was the Duc de Morny, half-brother to the Emperor. But he died and now once again Cora is under Royal patronage, so to speak."

Blanche paused and Linetta wondered exactly what was implied by the words, '*cher ami*'.

'Had Cora Pearl been engaged to the Duc de Morny?' she wondered.

It seemed unlikely that anyone who was Royal would be allowed to marry a commoner however rich she might be.

"Cora is always lucky," Blanche continued with just a touch of envy in her voice. "The Prince Napoleon has not only given her the key to the *Palais Royal* but has bought her two houses, the latest in the *Rue de Bassins*."

Linetta had no idea what was meant by this, so she asked tentatively,

"Who is the Prince Napoleon?"

"The Emperor's cousin," Blanche answered, "and one of the gayest, most irresistible and attractive men in all of Paris."

She gave a little sigh.

"Cora is so rich that her jewels alone are worth a million francs and her large dinners, masked balls and stupendous suppers are more sumptuous than any that the rest of us can offer."

There was no doubt now of the envy in Blanche's voice and Linetta asked,

"Is Miss Cora Pearl an actress?"

Blanche laughed.

"Two years ago she appeared at the *Théâtre des Bouffes Parisiens*, but she was not a success."

"Why not?" Linetta asked.

"She could not act. But she wore little else but diamonds! The buttons of her boots were large diamonds of the purest water and at the end of her performance she threw herself flat on her back and flung her legs in the air!"

"What for?" Linetta enquired.

"To show the audience that the soles of her boots were one mass of diamonds!"

Linetta gasped as Blanche finished,

"Now she has her box at the theatre and is content to criticise those who can really act."

Linetta had the chance to judge Blanche's acting ability for herself later that evening.

They returned from the *Bois de Boulogne* with time for Linetta to have a rest of half an hour. Then in her new evening gown, which had arrived from Madame Laferrière, she waited in the hall until Blanche came downstairs to drive to the theatre.

As the closed carriage moved through the streets, Linetta could see the gas globes illuminating the crowds moving along the pavements. There were also brilliant displays of light outside the packed *cafés*.

Jet lights blazed on the corners of the theatre as Blanche alighted at the main door and there were cheers from those waiting outside. She smiled and waved to them and then swept into the big marble-paved vestibule.

Linetta had already learnt that Blanche disdained the stage door used by the other actors and always made her entrance through the auditorium. This enabled those who arrived early to have a glimpse of her before, as she put it herself, she 'undressed for her part'.

Walking behind her, Linetta saw that the auditorium now looked very different from the dark gloomy void it had been at rehearsal.

Now the house was glittering. Tall jets of gas illuminated the great crystal pendant that hung from the arched dome with a stream of yellow and rose light.

The crimson plush of the seats that had appeared so dingy in the morning now looked rich and luxurious as a ruby.

The gold ornamentation shone and even the crude paintings on the ceiling appeared to be artistic.

Now the stage was draped in heavy purple curtains and made a palatial richness. The musicians were tuning up their instruments and the spectators ceased talking and jostling at Blanche's appearance to give her a clap and a cheer.

Linetta noticed that there was a great number of men standing in the stalls. They wore low-cut waistcoats, had a gardenia in their buttonholes and every gloved hand held an Opera glass to ensure that they would be able to study Blanche more closely.

Linetta had already been told that she was to sit in the stage box with Mr. Bischoffsheim. It was between high columns draped with long-fringed pelmets.

When she joined him, he rose and arranged the best seat in the front for her so that she would miss nothing of the performance.

She looked around her. The footlights were now lit and the audience were settling themselves, but the bustle and noise of their voices had increased.

The overture began and late arrivals compelled whole rows to stand up to let them pass, there was a shout from the depths of the pit and cries of '*hush*' from the galleries.

Linetta felt a thrill of expectation and sensed that the audience was experiencing it too. They were all waiting, as she was, to see Blanche!

"This is very – exciting," Linetta whispered to Mr. Bischoffsheim feeling that she should show that she was appreciative.

"It is your first visit to a French theatre?" he asked.

"My first visit to any theatre in the evening," Linetta replied. "But I have been to two afternoon performances of Shakespeare's plays."

Mr. Bischoffsheim looked amused and remarked dryly,

"You will find this somewhat different."

It was so different that Linetta, thinking back, was still bemused and confused by the whole performance.

The Operetta was, in her mind, very romantic and thrilling.

Then, when she saw Blanche making her triumphant appearance as Frédégonde, she could hardly believe it possible that anyone could appear in public wearing so little.

To say that she was shocked would be to underestimate what she felt. Blanche wore in fact less than when she had stepped from her bed that morning in her diaphanous nightgown.

The only difference was that she glittered.

There were diamonds everywhere. In her ears, round her neck, in her hair and Linetta could understand why, as the evening progressed, the whole theatre vibrated to the tumultuous applause.

Blanche not only looked like a glass of frothy champagne, she sparkled and she was intoxicated just by being herself.

She seemed, as she had done at rehearsal, to light up the whole theatre with her exuberance and vitality and in some way specially her own to include familiarly with the audience in her act.

Half-naked, singing, although Linetta realised again how little voice she had, she gaily threw in the hero's face the diamonds and the jewelled belt that he had given her.

Under the brilliance of the lights she appeared even more like a lascivious pink and white Goddess who had stepped out of a picture or down from some painted ceiling in an Emperor's Palace.

When the performance was over, great baskets of flowers and bouquets were carried onto the stage as Blanche took call after call from an enraptured audience.

They had then driven back with Mr. Bischoffsheim to the *Avenue de Friedland* and, although it seemed to Linetta very late at night, there was a dinner party.

There had been no time since her arrival for Linetta to examine the rest of the house, but now she saw the big drawing room, which was decorated in over-rich Louis XV style.

Four white marble female figures with bare bosoms held standard lamps. There were bronzes and Chinese *cloisonné* vases filled with flowers.

The lofty dining room, adorned with Gobelin tapestries boasted a huge monumental sideboard covered with ancient silver plate and the table was illuminated by silver candelabra, each holding fifteen candles.

It was also decorated with baskets of orchids and a number of gold ornaments, while the champagne sparkled in silver gilt goblets, each fashioned in the shape of an animal's head.

There was, however, little time to notice the background for the rooms filled rapidly with guests who had come on from the theatre.

Linetta was introduced to them, but she was long past hearing anyone's name or remembering it.

The men in their tailcoats with a large expanse of white shirtfront seemed to her to be all very impressive and the women might, she reflected, have all posed for pictures of Goddesses or *Bacchantes*.

It took her a little time to realise that their pink and white perfection, the darkness of their long eyelashes and the crimson of their lips were owed to cosmetics.

She had never before seen women painted, but she accepted that it was a Parisian fashion and she should not compare it with the unadorned severity of the English ladies she had known.

Behind every chair in the dining room there was a footman with powdered hair and in knee breeches wearing what she had learnt was Blanche's special livery of bright blue with silver braid.

The food was, as Linetta was assured by the gentleman sitting on her left, superlative, but she was too inexperienced to be discriminating. She only knew that it was delicious.

Vodka was served with *blinis* and caviar.

"This is the only house I ever visit where I am offered enough caviar," a middle-aged man, who Linetta had vaguely realised was a Duc, remarked.

He had three helpings, while Linetta, who had never tasted caviar before, took one tiny portion and ate it rather carefully.

After a *terrine de foie gras*, Linetta was offered a dish of what she learnt was lobster and peacock in galantine.

'Peacock!" she exclaimed. "How could anyone eat such a magnificent bird?"

"It's a delicacy, my dear," the Duc replied, "and delicacies, like our hostess, are expensive but our host can well afford them both."

Linetta looked to the end of the long table and realised that Mr. Bischoffsheim was presiding over the dinner while Blanche sat at the other end facing him.

"I will say one thing for Bischoffsheim," the Duc went on, talking, Linetta could not help feeling, more to himself than to her, "he can choose a good wine. This *Château Yquem* is excellent and I shall be surprised if we do not follow it with *Château Lafite*."

Numerous crystal glasses engraved with Blanche's initials were filled beside Linetta's plate, but she only sipped at one occasionally because she felt thirsty. When the glasses were removed, hers were still three quarters full.

As the dinner progressed and the animal heads of stag, fox, wolf and boar were filled and refilled with champagne, the voices of the guests grew louder and their laughter seemed to ring out continuously.

It seemed to Linetta watching that the ladies in the party were flirting quite openly with the gentlemen on either side of them.

The décolletages of their elaborate dresses were very low and if ever they bent forward she blushed at how much was revealed.

Sometimes she would catch a sentence of conversation that appeared to be serious and once she heard the names 'Houssaye' and 'Banville' and had the idea that they were writers.

The dinner seemed to go on for hours.

At the end, enhanced by marsala, malmsby and sherry came *fraises au kirsch, napolitains* and *mille-feuilles Pompadour.*

Then with the coffee, to Linetta's absolute astonishment, not only did the gentlemen light cigars but Blanche and several other of the women smoked cigarettes!

Never had she imagined in the whole of her life that she would ever see a woman smoking.

It was easy for her to watch the smoke-blowing beauties without their being aware of it, because everybody except herself seemed to be deep in conversation.

There were conversations punctuated with laughter and kisses bestowed on a white hand or words whispered into a small, heavily be-diamonded ear.

It was Mr. Bischoffsheim who realised that Linetta was not only silent but also very sleepy.

He was walking from his place at the end of the table towards Blanche when he stopped to lay a hand on her shoulder.

"You have had a long day, child," he said. "If you take my advice you will slip away and go to bed. There is always tomorrow."

"Thank you – I am feeling very sleepy," Linetta admitted.

"Then *dormez bien*," he said kindly.

As he walked away, Linetta rose to her feet. No one appeared to notice that she was leaving and, when she reached the door, she looked back.

Mr. Bischoffsheim was standing behind Blanche's chair and, as she watched, he bent forward and kissed the nakedness of her white shoulder.

It was a gesture that would have surprised Linetta had she seen it happen when they were alone, but in the middle of a large dinner party it astonished her to the point that she stood at the door staring, her eyes very wide.

Then she noticed that Mr. Bischoffsheim was not the only gentleman bestowing his caresses on the attractive ladies in their low cut gowns.

Because what she saw embarrassed her, Linetta slipped from the dining room and ran upstairs to her bedroom.

Now in the darkness of her room she thought over what she had seen and knew that not only her mother would have been shocked but also Mademoiselle.

She had spoken of Marie-Ernestine as her quiet, gentle well-behaved niece who loved the country.

How could she have guessed for one moment that this beautiful sensational actress could be the Marie-Ernestine she had known and loved?

Then Linetta told herself that she must not be censorious. This was not only the world of the theatre which she knew nothing about, it was also Paris!

French people were different from the stolid, sober self-controlled English.

'Mama was French, but she came from Normandy,' she told herself. 'What is more, she lived in England nearly all of her life.'

At the same time it was all very puzzling.

Linetta wished that there was someone who could explain it all to her and tell her too what part she should play in this strange fascinating life, which until today she had not known existed.

She thought of the gowns hanging in her wardrobe and the others that Blanche had ordered for her, of the fine silk underclothes, the satin slippers, the expensive gloves and reticules.

She possessed a whole wardrobe that must have cost a fortune and which she had received because Blanche was kind to her and Mr. Bischoffsheim was generous.

Yet such an extravagant gift made Linetta feel uneasy.

She was sure that she should not have accepted such a magnificent present from a stranger and yet what was the alternative?

It was all so difficult to understand and impossible to sort out in her tired mind.

She had a feeling that, if she could talk to somebody like the Marquis, he would tell her what she should do and what was right and what was wrong.

At the thought of him she could visualise him quite vividly walking towards the Steamer, smiling at her in the cabin and finding her a compartment on the train.

She had indeed felt safe and protected when she was with him.

What was more, it was impossible to forget his handsome face, his height, his broad shoulders and the athletic way that he moved.

'There was not a man at the party tonight who looked as distinguished or elegant as he did just in his travelling clothes,' Linetta told herself and wondered if she would see him again or if he would even remember her.

The theatre, the party and even her new clothes were forgotten as she fell asleep thinking about the Marquis.

*

As a matter of fact the Marquis had thought of Linetta not once but several times during the day.

When the train had arrived at the *Gare du Nord*, he had sent his valet to help with her luggage and find out if her friends had met her as he expected them to do.

The valet had returned to say that Linetta's carriage was empty and there was no sign of the young lady.

'I expect she was met and her friends hurried her away quickly,' the Marquis decided.

At the same time he found himself several times during the day thinking of Linetta's childlike appearance and the fear that had been in her eyes when she had come to his cabin.

'She should not have been travelling alone,' he mused and tried to dismiss the whole episode from his mind. But somehow it was impossible.

He found himself hoping that she would not be spoilt too quickly in Paris. There had been something ingenuous and spring-like about her that he had not often found in the young women he encountered in Society.

He had, however, a great deal to do.

Before he left England the Prime Minister, Mr. William Gladstone, had asked him to call on him at No. 10 Downing Street.

The Marquis had not been surprised because before he had inherited the title he had been a member of the Diplomatic Service and on several occasions his knowledge of European countries had been of service to the Prime Minister of the day.

Mr. Gladstone had formed a Government the previous year when in the General Election the Liberals were returned with a large majority.

At sixty Mr. Gladstone was tall with a strong profile, firm mouth, thin lips and a prominent chin. He had phenomenal energy, which enabled him to work as much as sixteen hours a day.

As an orator he could sway the House of Commons or a public meeting.

Mr. Gladstone's dominant characteristics were love of religion and love of right. He was modest and continually ascribed his successes to a higher Power.

The Marquis admired him for his sincerity and sense of purpose.

"I hear you are thinking of going to France, Darleston," the Prime Minister said after he had greeted the Marquis.

"Yes, Prime Minister."

"Then I want you to do something for me," Mr. Gladstone said bluntly.

The Marquis inclined his head.

"It will be a pleasure."

"You know Paris well and you are, I understand, a friend of the Emperor."

The Marquis had no need to answer.

Mr. Gladstone was not asking a question, he was merely stating a fact.

"I have a feeling," the Prime Minister went on, "that France is nearing a crisis."

"You are thinking they might go to war again?" the Marquis ventured.

"Exactly," the Prime Minister agreed. "Since the battle of Sadowa, when Prussia defeated Austria, the Balance of Power in Europe has changed. France is now well aware of the Prussian challenge to her grandeur."

"I heard," the Marquis interposed, "that the French Press has begun to stir up warlike feeling. It would be difficult for any French Government to watch idly while Prussia unites Germany."

"That is what our Ambassador tells me," Mr. Gladstone said. "At the same time the Emperor is sixty-one and in bad health. Can he really wish for war?"

"Not the Emperor," the Marquis replied quietly, "but the Empress!"

"That is exactly what I want you to find out for certain," Mr. Gladstone exclaimed. "I am told that the Emperor is being pushed not only by his wife but also by his Foreign Minister, the Duc de Grammont. But I want to hear the inside story, which I feel you, and you alone, will be able to find for me."

"I will do my best, Prime Minister."

"Send me anything you learn through the Diplomatic Bag," the Prime Minister told him, "and thank you, Darleston, for promising me your assistance."

Before the Marquis left the Prime Minister had given him confidential reports on all the main figures in the French Government and in the Emperor's direct entourage.

The majority were in his judgment accurate, although he found that he knew far more about many of the social personalities than did the minor Diplomats, who had compiled the reports so laboriously in the Foreign Office.

While the Prime Minister might consider him a friend of the Emperor, he was in fact a far closer associate of the Prince Napoleon, who was considered to be the most controversial, gifted and significant figure of the Second Empire.

As an Imperial Highness and a Senator, the Prince's political beliefs were a considerable problem to his cousin and at all times as controversial as his speeches.

Marshal Canrobert had refused to give him command of the assault troops at the Battle Sebastopol I the Crimea and, annoyed by this and the indecisive conduct of the whole campaign, Prince Napoleon had left the Crimea and returned to Paris.

He was accused of cowardice and his childhood name of *'Plon Plon'* was changed to *'Craint-plomb'*.

The imputation did not appear to upset him nor did it alter his publicly proclaimed dislike of the Empress and his independence of the Emperor.

But his private life became even more flamboyant than it had been in the past. His mistresses were legion and he flaunted them in full view of Paris.

His wife, the dull, virtuous and exceedingly religious Princess Clotilde, who had borne him three children, was constantly engaged in good works and was endlessly charitable and forgiving.

"She is the most saintly woman I have ever met," someone had said once to the Marquis, "but the Prince remains in effect what he prefers to be, a bachelor. In the morning there is always some or other petticoat trailing in his private apartments."

It was through his friendship with the Prince Napoleon that the Marquis had met, when he first went to Paris, the *Demi Monde* that had made the Second Empire the *'Golden Era of the Courtesans'*.

In Paris there was a dozen who were generally known as *'La Garde'* who were *expertes des sciences galantes* and Queens of their profession.

Each one of these *grandes cocottes* had amassed vast fortunes and possessions that made even the treasures in the Tuilleries fade into insignificance.

"When I have been to your *hotel*," Alfonse de Rothschild said to one of them, "my own *hotel* seems like a hovel to me."

'*Hotel*' was the French word for a large private townhouse, such as the mansions occupied by '*Les Grandes Horizontales*' as the *cocottes* were called.

Whenever the Marquis was in Paris he renewed his acquaintance with La Païva, perhaps the richest and most fantastic of them all. Her main lover was Herchel von Donnesmarck, who was well known to Bismarck and she was, the Marquis knew, certainly intriguing with the Prussians.

La Païva, who was Russian by birth, hated France because she felt that it had insulted her during her climb to fame. She therefore made every effort to make her house in the *Champs Élysées* a centre of Prussian espionage.

The Marquis told himself that it would be interesting to hear from La Païva what she thought of the present situation, just as he had every intention of calling on Cora Pearl.

The English member of *La Garde,* Cora's chain of lovers had included the Prince of Orange, Heir to the Throne of the Netherlands and she was now, the Marquis was well aware, the mistress of Prince Napoleon.

Not only because of the Marquis's rank was he *persona grata* with the *Demi Monde* as well as with the Royal household, but also because his charm and his Diplomatic training had opened most doors to him wherever he went.

He knew, however, that it would be correct for him first to pay his respects to the Emperor and he had already informed the Grand Marshal of the Palace, Maréchal Vaillant, that he was arriving in Paris.

He was therefore not surprised to find an invitation to dinner with the Emperor on the night he arrived.

It was not an engagement that the Marquis looked forward to with much enthusiasm.

Dinner in the Tuilleries was served at half past seven. At seven-twenty when Napoleon III and the Empress made their appearance in the *Salon des Tapisseries*, the Marquis was waiting with the Emperor's *aide-de-camp*, his Chamberlain, his Equerry, his Orderly Officer, the Prefect of the Palace, and two Ladies-in-Waiting.

The Emperor greeted him with pleasure and the Empress was gracious but slightly frigid.

When dinner was served, the *Maître d'Hôtel* informed the Prefect of the Palace who made a low bow to the Emperor.

Napoleon offered his arm to his wife and preceded by the Prefect they went into the dining room.

When the meal was informal as it was tonight, the Marquis being an intimate friend, the Prince Imperial was present.

From the age of eight he had been allowed to join his parents for dinner. It was a doubtful pleasure, as he much preferred to be with his goldfish and his magic lantern.

Besides the Prince Imperial there were two younger cousins of the Emperor and a Spanish friend of the Empress who had recently arrived from Spain.

The table, as usual, groaned under *Louis Seize* silver baskets filled with flowers from *Bourjon*, the local florist.

There were silver candelabra and on silver stands plates of *petits fours, compotiers* and dishes of fruit.

The soup and dessert plates were also silver and on other silver stands there were the two main dishes and four *entrées* before they were removed to be carved.

The Empress had in attendance her Nubian servant, Scander. In his gold-embroidered robes he looked like an exotic figure from some eighteenth century painting.

He brought that theatrical note to the proceedings that made the Marquis always feel in the Tuilleries as if he was performing on the stage.

There was, however, no doubt that for the Marquis as well as everyone else the evening was two and a half hours of unrelieved boredom.

The Emperor wanted to talk at dinner, but there was in fact little that he could say. Politics, whether internal or international were forbidden subjects in front of the servants.

Art and Literature, as the Marquis knew, were not considered socially acceptable and anyway neither the Emperor nor the Empress knew much about them.

The meal, chosen by the Adjutant General of the Palace, General Rollin, was dull, unimaginative and, as someone had once described it, 'the simple, plentiful and slightly dated cooking of a conscientious hotel'.

When it ended, the party repaired to the salon.

Now at last the Emperor could draw the Marquis aside and talk to him without being overheard.

"Tell me about London," His Majesty urged him.

There was an eagerness in his voice that made the Marquis realise that he was sometimes homesick for the free life that he had enjoyed in England when he was in exile.

He had been without money except what he could beg or borrow, but nevertheless he had been free of the confining Pomp and Ceremony that he often found irksome now that he was in power.

The Marquis, knowing what was expected of him, talked of the friends that the Emperor had made in the Clubs of St. James's Street and of Queen Victoria, who had found him fascinating and gradually brought the subject round to what he wished to know himself.

"I find that France is enjoying both prosperity and peace, Sire," he remarked.

He thought that the Emperor's expression darkened.

"For the moment."

"We are hoping in England it will be forever."

The Emperor shrugged his shoulders and it was, the Marquis thought, an expression of helplessness.

"The Duc de Grammont speaks warningly of the rising Military power of Prussia."

"I feel, Sire," the Marquis ventured, "that France should not suffer from any more wars at this moment in her history."

"That is what I think," the Emperor agreed. "In war no one wins, no-one!"

There was no chance to say anything more as it was nearly ten o'clock and the Marquis was expected to take his leave. But he had heard what he had expected. He knew that the Emperor, as the Prime Minister had thought, had no wish for war, but there was every chance that he might be pushed into one.

The servants had brought tea into the salon and the Marquis accepted a cup that was poured out by the Empress. Then thankfully he was able to escape.

The Duc de Rochfort was taking him to a party given by one of the *Grandes Cocottes*, Léonide Leblanc, who had earned the title of 'Madame Maximum' from the number of lovers she had accommodated.

She was exquisitely beautiful, witty, good-natured, amusing, very ambitious and very *intrigante* and she had brought *la galanterie* up to a fine art.

The party was to be given in the *Grand Seize*, the celebrated Room 16 at the *Café Anglais*. Léonide's guests would include the loveliest women in Paris and the most notorious men-about-town or *noceurs*.

There would be *baccarat* to amuse them and perhaps Léonide would act in a short sketch with Sarah Bernhardt or maybe Adelina Patti would sing.

Léonide was not only an actress she had also written a book, which had gone into three editions within a year. Her current lover was the Duc d'Aumale and she had Georges Clemenceau at her feet as well.

Yes, the Marquis told himself, he was looking forward to the evening now that he had done his duty at the Tuilleries!

Yet, as he drove towards the *Café Anglais*, he found himself once again thinking of Linetta,

He wondered what the friends she was staying with were like and what side of life in Paris she would see.

He would be spending his time partly with the famous and partly with the infamous!

He was sure that Linetta would move in a very different type of Society. The upper middle class, or those who belonged to the *ancien regime*, were very strict and unbending in their attitude towards the new Society.

In a way the Marquis was sorry that he had not questioned Linetta further. It would be, he thought, interesting to find out her reactions.

Then he told himself that he had wasted enough thought on a girl he had encountered just briefly on the journey.

And yet oddly enough he could see her small heart-shaped face very clearly and the expression in her large blue-grey eyes as she asked if she could stay with him for a few moments.

'Someone should have accompanied her,' he said to himself once again.

Why should it still trouble him that she was so vulnerable to the insults of those who would find her lovely face irresistible?

*

When Linetta awoke in the morning, it was to find that it was still quite early by French standards.

The maid who had helped her to undress when she had gone to bed after the dinner party had asked her whether she would like her *petit déjeuner* at nine o'clock or if she would prefer to ring when she woke up.

"At nine o'clock?" Linetta questioned. "Surely everyone is awake before that?"

"Not Madame," the maid replied with a smile.

"I expect she will be late," Linetta reflected.

"Madame seldom goes to bed before two or three o'clock in the mornin'," the maid explained, "and she enjoys her sleep. You'll not see her, *m'mselle,* before ten o'clock and probably later."

She saw Linetta's look of surprise and added,

"This morning was an exception. Madame retired to bed last night immediately after she came back from the theatre. It was most unusual."

Finally Linetta had agreed that the maid should bring her coffee and *croissants* at half-past nine.

She was actually awake at eight o'clock and feeling that it was impossible to lie quietly in bed she rose to draw back the curtains and look out at the sun shining over the roofs of Paris.

The house had a small garden at the back, which Linetta could see was bright with flowers.

She wondered if it would disturb anybody if she dressed and went downstairs before breakfast to walk in the garden. Then she felt too nervous to do so.

The servants would certainly not be expecting her. She remembered when the footman had first opened the door that he had not been wearing his coat.

Besides there was always the chance that she might disturb Blanche and that, she was quite sure, would be very unacceptable to her hostess.

She therefore dressed but stayed in her bedroom until her breakfast was brought to her with the news that Blanche was awake and would like to see her in a quarter of an hour.

Wearing the pretty gown that Madame Laferrière had dressed her in the day before, Linetta went to Blanche's bedroom to find her looking very beautiful as she sat up in her fantastic bed.

When Linetta appeared, she pushed aside her coffee and *croissants*.

"Come and sit down," she invited, her voice gay and lilting. "I have a friend coming this morning whom I want you to meet. She was at dinner last night and she said that she would call early so that we could talk over your future."

"It is very kind of you to take so much trouble," Linetta replied. "I have been thinking of what I could do and, although you are against my teaching, I feel that is in fact the only thing that I am qualified to do."

"Marguerite Bellanger will have very different ideas, I am sure," Blanche said confidently. "You will like her. She is very beautiful and very sweet. She is one of the few real friends I have where women are concerned."

"What does she do?" Linetta asked, thinking that she might be an actress as well.

There was a moment's silence and she had the feeling that Blanche was wondering how she should reply.

Then she answered,

"Marguerite gives the most delightful parties. I feel sure that she will ask you to one and you will enjoy yourself."

What Blanche had decided not to tell Linetta was that Marguerite Bellanger had been the Emperor's mistress until the Empress had persuaded her to give him up.

The story of their meeting was very romantic.

Marguerite, who came from a humble background, came to Paris to try out her dramatic talents in a play by Dumas Père in the little theatre in the *Rue de la Tour d'Auverge*.

She was not a success. She was gauche and the audiences were noisy and critical. Turning to face them Marguerite shouted out,

"*Zut!*"

She abandoned her stage career and by 1862 had become a *cocotte* of the second rank. She was beautiful, robust, gay and, like Blanche, radiated vitality and health.

One day she was sheltering from the rain at St. Cloud.

She had followed a lover there who was attached to the Royal Household, when the Emperor, passing in his carriage, saw her.

Thinking her attractive he threw her a tartan rug.

The next day Marguerite requested an audience with His Majesty, claiming that she had an urgent personal message for him.

The Emperor was fascinated by the request and that very day Marguerite became his mistress. She delighted a rather jaded and bored Emperor by her tomboyish ways and her refreshing gaiety.

After the stiff etiquette of the Court, he found himself enjoying her spontaneity and naturalness and their liaison continued for nearly two years.

Through his secretary the Emperor bought her a small hotel in the *Rue de Vignes* at Poissy and often visited her there.

Marguerite soon set up a salon that was almost a Court and the gravest as well as the most frivolous persons were among her guests. There were Ministers, Senators, Equerries, Chamberlains, actors, Diplomats, soldiers, writers and buffoons!

Marguerite enjoyed every moment of it.

She had her writing paper embossed with a silver-petalled gold-centred marguerite and the motto, '*All things come to those who wait*'.

But the position she held went to her head.

She followed the Emperor to Vichy and once in broad daylight she arrived by carriage at his chalet where he was presiding over a Council of Ministers.

She then went to Biarritz and, when the Court moved to St. Cloud, she lived in a little house that adjoined the Private Park and there was a hidden door in the wall that the Emperor used.

The Empress, having discovered that her husband's liaison was far from casual, began to get annoyed and she was not the only person.

The Courtiers and Statesmen were certain that the Emperor's secretary, Mocquard, used Marguerite as a means of influencing the Emperor.

In October 1864 the Emperor was brought home in a state of collapse from Marguerite's house in the *Rue de Vignes* and the Empress then decided that the liaison must end.

France could no longer afford to have a Ruler who endangered his health with a *Grande Cocotte*.

The Empress visited Marguerite, told her that she was killing the Emperor and insisted that she must give him up. By the beginning of 1865 one of the Empress's *confidantes* wrote to a friend,

"*Caesar thinks no more of Cleopatra*".

However, those who knew Paris intimately were aware that in February 1864 a child had been born in Marguerite's house. He was registered as *Charles-Jules-Augustus-François-Marie, father and mother unknown.*

Among the four signatures on the document was a friend of the Emperor's cousin. Princess Mathilde.

When Marguerite's love affair with the Emperor was over, she had accumulated a large fortune, a *hotel* in Paris, a Château in the country and a great number of ardent admirers.

There was no doubt that being the last important mistress of the Emperor enveloped her with an aura of glamour that remained with her all her life.

It was, however, Blanche thought, not the sort of story that she should relate at this moment to Linetta.

It was impossible not to realise how very innocent and unsophisticated the girl was.

When Marguerite Bellanger arrived, she was beautifully dressed, although her gown was not as fantastic as those affected by Blanche.

But at the same time, Blanche told herself, sooner or later she would have to wake up to the facts of life. That was why she had asked Marguerite to come in this morning to discuss her future.

At twenty-nine she was at the height of her beauty and she still had the gay uninhibited frankness that had attracted the Emperor. Her smile was warm and spontaneous so that everyone instinctively felt friendly towards her.

"Blanche has been telling me all about you," Marguerite said to Linetta. "You have come to Paris at just the right time. Everything is so amusing!"

As she spoke, she took off her elegant hat with its fluttering feathers and sat down in a comfortable chair.

She looked very French and fashionable but equally she had a youthful air about her that made Linetta feel that she was almost a girl like herself.

"I told you last night," Blanche joined in from the bed, "that we had to discuss Linetta's future. My aunt sent her to me and naturally I want to do what is in her best interests."

"But, of course, Blanche, and it is so like you to take other people's troubles on your shoulders," Marguerite replied.

She turned to Linetta again,

"There is no one kinder or more generous than Blanche. She cannot see a dog starving in the street without crying over it and she will take the fur from her shoulders to give it to a poor child."

"She has been very kind to me," Linetta said in a soft voice.

"You will find that a great number of people in Paris will want to be kind to you," Marguerite continued enigmatically.

"Linetta keeps telling me," Blanche interposed, "that she must earn her living by teaching English. Can you imagine anything more depressing or more frustrating than coping with other people's children?"

Marguerite gave a little sigh.

"So different from one's own."

"How is Charles?" Blanche asked.

Marguerite's eyes lit up.

"He is quite entrancing. He was five years old two months ago. One day when you can spare the time I will bring him to see you."

"I would like that," Blanche enthused.

"Perhaps I could teach your little boy English?" Linetta suggested.

Marguerite shook her head.

"It's quite enough to get him to speak French properly. The people who look after him have engaged a *bonne* who comes from Provence. She is an excellent woman but oh, the strange expressions she uses! And her accent! I assure you, it's deplorable."

Linetta did not like to press the point that she could alter this and Marguerite, as if she was determined to concentrate on her rather than her son, said to Blanche,

"I was watching Linetta last night. Do you realise lovely she is/ Far lovelier than most of our friends."

"That is what I thought," Blanche agreed, "and it is a different sort of beauty and unique in its way."

"Her nose is aristocratic," Marguerite went on. "Her eyes are pools of mystery and her hair is like spring sunshine."

Linetta looked shy and then realised that there was a smile on Blanche's face and on Marguerite's.

"I imagine that we are thinking of the same thing," Blanche murmured finally.

"Shall I put it into words or will you?" Marguerite enquired.

"I think you will make it clearer than I shall be able to do," Blanche replied. "After all we have to persuade her that it is the best possible solution where she is concerned."

There was something in the way they spoke that made Linetta feel apprehensive.

"What is – it?" she asked. "What are you planning – for me?"

Marguerite hesitated a moment and then she responded,

"You are too pretty, Linetta, to find employment in Paris. For one thing no lady would engage you to teach her children."

"But why not?" Linetta asked.

"Because you would undoubtedly attract not only the sons of the household but also the Master and perhaps Madame's own particular beau!"

"But that is absurd," Linetta protested.

"Unfortunately it is the truth. Perhaps things are different in England, but in France, even if you obtained employment in a private house, I doubt if you would remain there longer than a week!"

Linetta looked at Blanche in consternation.

"Is that – true?" she asked.

"Marguerite knows what she is talking about," Blanche replied. "She has moved with the very best people in the land."

Marguerite gave her an amused smile.

"That is true and therefore let me tell you, Linetta, that there is only one way of life open to you."

"And what is – that?"

"You must become," she said slowly, "and it will be very easy with your looks, *une Grande Cocotte!*"

Linetta's eyes were growing wide and then wider.

"What is that?" she asked. "I don't think – I have ever heard of it."

CHAPTER FOUR

There was a sudden silence and Blanche's eyes met Marguerite's.

"You explain to her," Blanche proposed softly.

She lay further back against her lace-trimmed pillows, watching Linetta's face.

The girl was lovely, too lovely perhaps for the life they were suggesting for her, but at least with Marguerite's and her help Linetta would start at the top.

She would not have to go through the misery that she had experienced when at fourteen a young shop assistant had taken her to the *Closerie de Lilas*.

There in the gas lit pleasure gardens, excited by the wine and exotically conflicting smells of scent and cigars, she had danced the *Can-Can*.

Her escort had vanished and left her to drink champagne with some of his friends. One of them, a Wallachian, seduced her and a few weeks later had taken her to Bucharest.

Blanche could remember all too vividly the disreputable inn where they had stayed. She also grew to dislike her lover and then ran away.

She joined some gypsy minstrels and danced to their violins and mandolins, but because she was not one of them they ill-treated her and again she ran off on her own.

Somehow, perhaps because as she believed that her Guardian Angel looked after her, she had met a Prince, who fell in love with her and introduced her to top Wallachian Society.

She had gone back to Paris like a homing pigeon and from then on everything she touched turned to gold!

But how long would it last? Blanche crossed her fingers, at heart she was still a superstitious peasant girl from her native Indre.

It was not only money that mattered, she thought to herself now, although it made life very comfortable, happiness was more important and because she herself was always happy she wanted to please everyone she came into contact with.

Marguerite was watching Linetta's face too and, choosing her words very carefully, she began in a gentle voice,

"You know that in France marriages are arranged and there is no question of a gentleman having a choice of brides. It is his father who decides who will be a suitable *parti*."

"Mama told me all about that," Linetta replied. "It does not happen – in England."

She was thinking of how very much in love her mother had been with her father. Theirs had very obviously not been a *mariage de convenance*.

"Royal marriages are arranged," Marguerite contradicted, "and I have always heard that the aristocracy, the Noblemen of England, follow the example of their Monarchy."

"Yes – I suppose that is – true," Linetta admitted hesitatingly.

"Then you can understand that in France a man who is married to a bride who he has not chosen for himself, longs to find love with a woman of his own choice."

Marguerite saw that Linetta was listening intently and she went on,

"That is why a man to all intents and purposes will take himself a 'second wife', someone he admires, someone he loves and someone he looks after and who he will spend a great deal of money on."

"It seems a trange – arrangement," Linetta commented nervously.

"But why?" Marguerite enquired. "Surely you would not expect any man to go through life without love, without romance and without a woman who he can give his heart to?"

There was a poignant silence and then Linetta asked in a low voice,

"Is – that what is – meant by a – *cocotte*?"

"Exactly," Marguerite approved. "But there are, you will understand, various grades and *Les Grandes Cocottes* are among the most important, the most admired and the most influential women in France!"

"Are you and Blanche – *Grandes Cocottes*?" Linetta asked.

"We are indeed," Marguerite replied. "And under our auspices you will join *La Haute Galanterie*."

"I think," Linetta said, "I would rather be – married properly."

Marguerite held up her hands as if in protest.

"And who do you think will marry you without a dowry and without any background?" she asked. "Besides, my dear child, all the men you are likely to meet will be married already. Their parents march them up the aisle almost as soon as they leave University or reach the age of twenty-one!"

"It seems – strange somehow," Linetta muttered uneasily.

"'You will get used to the idea," Blanche broke in, "and to have a *cher ami* who adores one, Linetta, makes life very easy. What is more one feels secure, looked after and protected."

At the word 'protected', Linetta thought of the Marquis.

He had protected her, she thought, and she had felt safe with him. Then what Blanche had said stuck a chord in her memory.

"Do you – mean," she asked, "that Mr. Bischoffsheim is *your – cher ami*?"

"But, of course, he is," Blanche replied. "He has loved me since he first saw me before I went to Russia and, when I returned, he bought me this house and has looked after me ever since."

That was what she now expected to hear, Linetta thought, seeing that Mr. Bischoffsheim had been the host at the party last night and Blanche had asked him if she could stay with her.

He had also paid for her clothes!

"Now don't worry," Marguerite said. "I promise you, Linetta, we are thinking of you and what is in your best interests. You are far too young to waste your life and your beauty teaching children or trying to find an English husband. Only a Frenchman appreciates a beautiful woman and is prepared to express his appreciation in diamonds."

Linetta clasped her hands together.

"You are quite – certain that it is not – wicked and – wrong?"

As she spoke she glanced at the ivory statue of Christ that Blanche had by her bedside.

"Not in France," Marguerite replied quickly, "and, when you get used to the idea, Linetta, you will realise that what Blanche and I are planning is for your own good."

"You are – very kind," Linetta said shyly.

There were so many other things she wanted to ask, but she felt that it was impossible to put them into words.

Marguerite had a child. What did his father think about that? And did he mind having a son who could not bear his name?

Even as she considered this, Linetta had a terrifying thought.

Could the reason for her using her mother's name and for her mother telling her so little about her father be that she was not his legitimate daughter?

Then she knew that this was a ridiculous idea.

Her mother had always worn her Wedding ring and, what was more, Linetta remembered her saying,

"My Wedding was the happiest and most spiritual moment of my life. I felt as if I was encompassed about by a company of angels."

Her mother would never have said that if it had been a lie. If she did not use her father's name, there must have been some good reason for it. She wished now that she had learnt it before her mother died.

In the meantime, as if there was nothing further to discuss, Blanche and Marguerite concerned themselves only with her appearance.

Blanche went off to the theatre for another rehearsal and Marguerite took Linetta shopping.

She had thought the day before that she had enough new clothes to last for a lifetime, but Marguerite had other ideas.

She took Linetta not to Madame Laferrière, but to the famous Monsieur Worth and ordered her three evening gowns and three day *toilettes*, which were so beautiful and so expensive that Linetta tried vainly to protest.

"One thousand two hundred francs is not really much for a gown," Marguerite replied at once.

"But I cannot ask Mr. Bischoffsheim to spend any more money on me, he only did it for Blanche's sake," Linetta cried.

"Mr. Worth will be in no hurry to have his account settled," Marguerite answered soothingly, "and it is not necessarily Mr. Bischoffsheim who will foot the bill."

Linetta looked at her nervously.

This meant that Marguerite was thinking of the *cher ami* she was to find herself, the man who was to protect her, look after her and to whom she would be a 'second wife'.

She kept feeling that her mother would not have approved and that Mademoiselle would surely never have heard of such a strange arrangement.

But what could she do?

If she refused to agree, Blanche might turn her away from the house and then where could she go?

Paris seemed very big and she knew that she would be frightened if she was alone in such a large City without friends.

She kept remembering the man on the ship who had pestered her with his attentions.

If the Marquis had not been there and she had not been able to escape to his cabin, what would have happened?

Linetta had no idea what a man expected of a woman.

She had been brought up without men in her life, in fact she had hardly had an opportunity of talking to one and certainly not alone.

And yet there were men like the traveller in the plaid cape who had forced himself upon her in a manner that had made her heart beat quickly and her mouth feel dry.

Surely rather than encounter that sort of situation again it would be better to have someone to look after her?

After all Mr. Bischoffsheim was not very attractive and he seemed rather old, but he was extremely kind and Blanche appeared to be happy with him.

Once again she found herself thinking of the Marquis and wishing that she could ask his advice. He was English and he had seemed so sane and sensible.

Supposing she could find him? Would he explain to her that what she was doing was correct and reasonable? Or would he tell her that she must refuse to do what Blanche and Marguerite were suggesting?

Marguerite took her back to luncheon at the house and Blanche arrived late from the theatre. She had decided to eat at home because she was having her hair washed in the afternoon.

"We will drive in the *Bois de Boulogne* as usual," she said, "but I suggest, Linetta, that until then you rest or read a book."

Linetta longed to explore Paris, but she realised that it would be impossible for her to do so alone and she did not like to ask if one of the servants could accompany her.

Marguerite kissed Linetta goodbye and left them.

"I will see you tomorrow or the next day," she said. "In the meantime I shall be thinking of you and trying to find exactly the right man to be your *cher ami*!"

"He might not – like me," Linetta stuttered in a worried voice.

"There are plenty of gentlemen who will like you," Marguerite laughed. "In fact Blanche and I will have to keep them at bay with a bargepole, but as your *duennas*, we intend to be very choosy and very very particular!"

She kissed Linetta again.

"You are a very sweet child. I hope you will not grow up too quickly."

Linetta did not understand what she meant by that.

'I suppose,' she told herself, 'it is because I am so ignorant and so inexperienced that they think of me as much younger than I am.'

Because Blanche expected it of her, she found a book and started towards her bedroom. Then changing her mind she went into the boudoir that Blanche had told her she could use whenever she liked.

Against a background of rose-coloured silk embroidered in gold thread, there was a multitude of objects from every country and in every style.

There were Spanish and Portuguese chests, miniature Chinese Pagodas, Japanese screens of precious workmanship, porcelain, bronzes, tapestries and *petit-point* besides large armchairs and two deep couches.

It was a strange room. It seemed to Linetta like an Aladdin's cave, at the same time as if the treasures in it had been collected by Blanche just because they were valuable and expensive and not particularly because she liked them.

There was another picture of her over the mantelpiece.

This one, painted by Manet, was not particularly flattering, but it was possible to see the likeness. It showed Blanche only half-dressed, wearing a blue corset and a short frilly petticoat, while she stood in front of a mirror with a powder puff in her hand.

'Why should she agree to be painted like that?' Linetta wondered.

She thought that the picture was somewhat vulgar when she noticed to her consternation that seated on a sofa behind Blanche there was depicted a gentleman in evening clothes wearing his top hat

He was staring at Blanche's blue corset with its pulled-in waist and to Linetta it seemed extremely immodest that she should allow herself to be watched by a man when she was not wearing a gown!

The book Linetta had intended to read remained unopened. She sat worrying and thinking about herself and about Blanche and Marguerite until it was time to drive in the *Bois de Boulogne.*

Today they used a caliche drawn by two fine piebald horses, its interior upholstered in a warm golden yellow, which echoed the colour of Blanche's hair.

She was resplendent in a yellow gown embroidered with topazes and her jewellery of topazes and diamonds seemed to hold the warmth of the sun.

Linetta wore white, her gown being trimmed with turquoise-blue ribbons and her hat with small feathers in the same colour.

She felt that she paled into insignificance beside Blanche. Yet she saw quite a number of gentlemen looking at her with what she was woman enough to know was a glint of admiration in their eyes.

The promenade did not take long and, when they returned to the house, Blanche sent her own *coiffeur* to Linetta's room to arrange her hair in the latest fashion with curls falling down the back of her head.

A new gown had arrived for her to wear that they had ordered the previous day. In white caught with bunches of snowdrops she looked very lovely and there were smaller bunches of the same flower to wear at the back of her head.

It was warm even in the evening, and the maid handed Linetta a wrap of chiffon trimmed with swansdown, which framed her shoulders like a white cloud.

"You look lovely!" Blanche exclaimed, coming down the stairs in another flamboyant gown, which made Linetta gasp. "Everyone will look at you in the box and no one will notice me on the stage!"

Linetta laughed.

"It is not what you wear," she replied, "it is because you are yourself that they applaud you."

"Thank you, that is a very nice compliment," Blanche smiled. "I must tell Bisch what you said. I often tell him that he is not poetical enough when he flatters me!"

They drove to the theatre and Linetta was delighted to see the *Opéra Bouffe* again. But she could not help wondering why Mr. Bischoffsheim did not get bored if he saw it every evening.

She was no sooner seated beside him in the stage box than the door behind them opened and a man's voice asked,

"May I join you, Raphael?"

Mr. Bischoffsheim rose to his feet.

"But, of course, Jacques," he replied.

A thin, rather cadaverous man had come into the box. He had a clever face, but Linetta, as she was introduced to him, thought that he must be as old if not older than Mr. Bischoffsheim.

"This is my friend, Jacques Vossin," Mr. Bischoffsheim said. "He is also a Banker and a very successful one."

The two men smiled at each other and Mr. Bischoffsheim offered Mr. Vossin a chair.

He sat down and the two men started to discuss stocks and shares in a low voice while Linetta concentrated on the stage.

Blanche was in even better form than she had been the night before and the audience applauded her rapturously and she was forced to take several curtain calls in the interval.

"I will go round and see her," Mr. Bischoffsheim announced. "You look after Linetta, Jacques. I will not be long."

He disappeared as the audience started to file from the auditorium into the vestibule where they could drink at the bars or at the white marble tables.

"You left the party early last night, *mademoiselle*," Mr. Vossin said to Linetta.

"I was sleepy because I had been travelling the night before," Linetta answered.

As she spoke, she tried to recall Mr. Vossin amongst Blanche's other guests, but he was one of those people, she thought, who was not particularly distinguishable.

He had dark hair and a sallow skin and his eyes, which looked tired, were deep-set above prominent cheekbones.

"You must have slept well," Mr. Vossin remarked.

"For a long time I was too excited to sleep. So much has happened to me, so much that was unexpected and yet it was all so wonderful!"

"I am glad that you like Paris," Mr. Vossin responded. "It's a very amusing City for those who know how to look in the right places."

He went on talking to Linetta, but she was not really listening. She found, now that the lights were up, that it was fascinating to watch the audience moving in and out of the stalls, leaving from the crowded dress circle and gallery.

Very modish ladies flashing with jewels were greeting their friends in the boxes opposite, but Linetta came to the conclusion that the women's gowns with their bustles and long trains were not really suited to the seats of a theatre.

"Do you agree?" she heard Mr. Vossin ask.

He broke in on her thoughts and she had no idea what the question had been.

"Oh – yes, of course," she answered.

Then the bell rang out to show that the interval was over and the people began crowding back into the auditorium.

Mr. Bischoffsheim returned with a smile on his lips.

"Blanche sends you her love," he said to Mr. Vossin. "She hopes you are enjoying the show."

"Could I do anything else, when Blanche is playing the lead?" Mr. Vossin enquired. "She is superb and magnificent, my dear Raphael. There is no one like her!"

Mr. Bischoffsheim looked pleased and proud.

The lights were dimmed and the curtain went up again.

When the *Opéra Bouffe* finished and Blanche was taking one curtain call after another while a mountain of flowers was being carried up onto the stage, Mr. Vossin turned to Linetta,

"I think we would be wise to slip away now. There will be such a congestion of carriages if we wait until everyone has left the theatre."

Linetta looked at him in astonishment.

"Are we not waiting for Blanche?"

"You promised you would have supper with me."

Linetta turned in consternation to Mr. Bischoffsheim.

"Go along with Jacques," he said good-humouredly. "If you want to join us later, he can bring you to the party that Caroline Letessier is giving tonight."

Linetta would have protested further, but Mr. Vossin took her arm and opened the door of the box.

"You are not being very tactful," he said in a low voice.

"Tactful?" Linetta questioned.

"I think my friend Raphael wishes to be alone with the lovely Blanche," he explained, "just as I am anxious to be alone with you."

His words made Linetta feel rather guilty.

Had she in fact imposed herself too much on Mr. Bischoffsheim's hospitality?

Now she thought of it, of course, he would want to be alone with Blanche and Blanche with her *cher ami*.

She had no wish to have supper alone with Mr. Vossin and she was quite certain that he would be something of a bore, but it was cheering to think that they could go on later to a party and find Blanche and Mr. Bischoffsheim there.

With an efficiency that she could not help admiring Mr. Vossin had his carriage brought to the front of the theatre only a few minutes after he had asked for it.

It was very comfortable and, as a warm sable rug was put over Linetta's knees, she remembered that Mr. Bischoffsheim had said that he was a very successful Banker.

'I suppose all Bankers are very rich,' she thought,

They drove off and Mr. Vossin said,

"I promised myself last night that I would take you out to supper at the first possible opportunity, but I was not optimistic enough to hope that it would happen quite so quickly!"

"Where are we going?" Linetta asked.

"To the *Café Anglais*," he replied. "Have you heard of it?"

"I think Blanche did mention it," Linetta said doubtfully. "Is the food very good?"

Mr. Vossin laughed.

"I should be extremely annoyed if it was not, because it is in fact the aristocratic Paris restaurant *par excellence.*"

"The food in France is so delicious that I feel if I stay here long I shall become very fat from overeating."

"I think it unlikely," Mr. Vossin replied. "But your figure is perfect as you must know. You are *une petite Venus* and I find you entrancing."

Because Linetta felt embarrassed by his compliment she said swiftly,

'Tell me about the *Café Anglais*."

"You shall see for yourself, but let me tell you that anyone with social or gastronomic pretensions feels obliged to go there immediately they arrive in Paris."

Linetta expected something very impressive, but found that the outside of the *Café Anglais* looked quite ordinary.

It was only when she entered that she found that it was not at all what she had expected, and that it had a strange individuality all its own.

The *Café Anglais* was in fact a labyrinth of vestibules and corridors leading to a succession of *cabinets particuliers*, private, mysterious and isolated rooms where you could dine *tête-à-tête* or *en famille*.

The most famous room was called the *Marivaux* and was also known as *Le Cabinet des Femmes du Monde*. To reach it, Society ladies hurried up a special staircase hoping that they would not be seen and recognised.

There was a restaurant in the cellar of the *Café Anglais*, which was known throughout Europe for its vast proportions and comfortable furnishings.

Its passages were sprinkled with sand and two hundred thousand bottles filled the recesses, while a miniature railway line ran silently bringing wine to each table.

On festive evenings countless bunches of different coloured grapes glowed under the vaults, along the pillars and in niches on the walls, making the cellar look like some vast Bacchic grotto.

But on entering the *Café Anglais*, Linetta saw nothing of this.

There was a crowd of people arriving in front of them and behind them, stepping out of expensive carriages, the women leaving a soft fragrance of expensive perfume on the air as they moved beside their escorts either into the restaurant or up one of the staircases.

Mr. Vossin stopped to talk to the *Maître d'Hôtel* and Linetta, looking into the restaurant, felt her heart give a sudden leap.

In the distance being shown to a table at the side of the room she could see the tall figure of the Marquis!

There was no mistaking his air of distinction or the proud way that he moved.

There were two men with him and Linetta hoped that they would be at a table where she could watch him while she ate supper with Mr. Vossin.

Then to her disappointment a waiter led them not into the restaurant but up a small staircase.

'I suppose the place is full,' Linetta told herself and she longed to ask Mr. Vossin to try again to find a table downstairs.

Then she told herself that he would think such behaviour ill-mannered and, if he was kind enough to give her supper, she should not argue about where he took her.

She was, however, astonished when the waiter opened the door of a small room. There was just one table laid for supper in the centre.

Linetta looked at Mr. Vossin and he explained quickly,

"It's so noisy downstairs that I thought it would be much easier for us to talk up here."

"Y-yes, of course," Linetta agreed reluctantly.

She could hardly say that she did not wish to talk to him and she would much rather be in the large restaurant, noisy though it might be.

She looked round the room. It was elegantly furnished with a large cushion-covered couch at one end.

Because she thought that there was nothing she could do but agree to what had been planned, Linetta took off her wrap and laid it on a chair by the door.

Then she sat down at the table while Mr. Vossin studied the menu.

She had learnt by now that one could not hurry a Frenchman when he was considering what he should eat.

A long discussion took place between Mr. Vossin and the *Maître d'Hôtel* before finally a large meal was ordered and then the wines in consultation with the *Sommelier*.

Waiters, who had brought in hot rolls, butter, dishes of shrimps, nuts and olives and laid them on the table, now left the room.

Mr. Vossin turned to Linetta with a smile.

"I have chosen what I think you will enjoy. As you are new to Paris, I thought that you would prefer me to order the specialities of this place, including the *écrevisses à la bordelaise*."

'That is very kind of you," Linetta said.

"I want to be kind," Mr. Vossin replied. "And may I say how honoured I am that the first time you should dine alone with anyone in Paris it should be with me."

"It is very kind of you to ask me."

Then, feeling that she must carry on the conversation' she added,

"I did not know that there were restaurants in Paris where one could dine privately like this."

"The French always cater for *l'amour*," Mr. Vossin replied. "You can imagine that these rooms have seen many different sorts of lovers over the years, some happy, some unhappy and many, of course, indulging in a clandestine affair."

Linetta wondered why, if it was a room for lovers, she and Mr. Vossin should dine in it.

Then she told herself that it was only because he was old and disliked noise that he had reserved a *cabinet particulier* rather than a table downstairs in the restaurant.

Waiters arrived with wine, which Mr. Vossin sampled very carefully and then the first course arrived and there was no need to talk except about the food, which was even more delicious than anything Linetta had ever tasted.

Dish succeeded dish, wine succeeded wine. Linetta drank little and found it impossible to eat everything that was put in front of her.

She was, however, fairly hungry because dinner was so late and also in France she missed the afternoon tea that she and her mother had always had at home at half-past four.

But even so after three courses she found herself unable to eat much more, while Mr. Vossin, despite the fact that he looked so thin, appeared to have an enormous appetite.

Finally the waiters served coffee and liqueurs, but while Linetta refused both, Mr. Vossin had a large brandy.

"Let's sit more comfortably on the sofa," he suggested to Linetta.

He rose from the table as he spoke. A waiter carried his glass of brandy and set it down on a small table beside the couch with its colourful silk cushions.

There was nothing that Linetta could do but join him.

She wondered as she did so how soon she could say that she would like to go home or on to the party where Mr. Bischoffsheim had suggested that they might join him and Blanche.

It seemed rather rude, she thought, to leave as soon as they had eaten, but she found Mr. Vossin difficult to talk to, which was not surprising. After all she knew little about banking and what could one say to a Banker anyway?

'Perhaps he owns racehorses as he is so rich,' she told herself and decided that to be polite she must find out what else interested him.

Because he expected it she sat down beside him on the couch.

He put out his hand and took hold of hers.

As he did so the waiters, having cleared the table, left the room.

"Now we can talk," Mr. Vossin began. "There is a great deal I want to know about you, Linetta."

She noticed the use of her Christian name and felt that it must be the fashion in France for everyone to be informal almost as soon as they met.

"I think you should tell me about yourself — first," she answered. "What are your interests?"

"My interest at the moment," he replied, "is you!"

Linetta started and looked at him in surprise. Then before she could move and before she could even speak, he put his arms round her waist and drew her closer to him.

"We are going to mean a great deal to each other," he murmured. "I am a very rich man, Linetta, and my fortune and my heart are both yours!"

As he spoke, his mouth came nearer to hers and she realised that he was about to kiss her.

With a little cry she turned her face away and his lips touched her cheek.

"No!" she cried. "No, *no!*"

The arm he had around her waist had drawn her closer to him and now with a violence that she had never used before Linetta fought herself free.

She rose to her feet before he could stop her and stood looking at him, her heart thumping and her mouth dry with fear.

"Now listen to me, Linetta," Mr. Vossin said. "I will give you everything you want – everything!"

He reached out his hand towards her, but, as he was about to touch her again, Linetta gave a little cry of sheer terror and ran away across the room.

He gave an amused laugh.

"If you want me to chase you, Linetta, I will do so, but I promise you I shall catch you in the end and I always get what I want."

There was no disguising the threat behind the words and Linetta saw that he was rising to his feet and knew that in the small confines of the room it would only be a few seconds before he did catch her.

It seemed to her for a moment that her brain was paralysed and she could not think what to do. Then, as if it was a lifeline, she saw her swansdown wrap lying on the chair near the door where she had put it.

It was the answer to the terror she felt within her and, snatching it up, she pulled open the door and without looking back ran down the narrow stairs.

As she reached the restaurant, she looked wildly across the room now filled to capacity.

Then she saw whom she was seeking.

Even as she identified the Marquis she thought that she heard Mr. Vossin calling her name from the top of the stairs.

Blindly and frantically she ran through the restaurant, pushing her way between the tables.

*

The Marquis had attended a Reception given by Princess Mathilde, the first cousin of the Emperor, and one of the most influential women in France.

She presided over a Salon that had been called *'the true Salon of the nineteenth century'*.

Princess Mathilde was the most distinguished hostess of the Second Empire and the Marquis had known that he would find in her house all the most senior Statesmen, as well as everyone in Paris who was cultured.

Painters, critics, poets, Ministers, Academicians were all to be found in the Princess's Salon and this evening the Marquis had been able to talk with a number of people who had contributed most usefully to the store of information that he was collecting for Mr. Gladstone.

The splendid rooms in the Princess's house in the *Rue de Courcelles* were filled with masterpieces of painting and furniture that would have graced the Louvre. There were also magnificent Conservatories.

But as always at huge Receptions it was difficult to find anything to eat and the Marquis had been only too willing to agree when the Duc de Rochfort had suggested that he and the Vicomte de Casablanca should go on to the *Café Anglais* for supper.

"Casablanca is always amusing," he said to the Marquis. "Moreover he has just returned from Bordeaux and he can tell you a great deal about the feeling in the Provinces regarding the Emperor and the Empress."

"That is what I want to hear," the Marquis replied.

Having thanked the Princess Mathilde for her hospitality they had driven in the Duc's comfortable carriage to the *Café Anglais*.

The Marquis was an old client and was greeted enthusiastically by the *Maître d'Hôtel* and sent his compliments to the chef.

Adolphe Dugléré was considered to be the greatest chef in Paris and it was said that all the other restaurants acknowledged him as an incomparable Master.

He was paid the princely salary of twenty-five thousand francs a year and was known to be very temperamental and overcome by emotion if he burnt a steak or curdled his sauces.

"I live in Paris," the Duc complained to the Marquis, "but I do *not* get the attention that you receive. I cannot understand it!"

"I was here two years ago," the Marquis replied, "when the Czar of Russia with the Czarevitch, the King of Prussia and Bismarck, who had come to visit the International Exhibition, all dined in *La Grande Seize.*"

"I have always been told," the Duc said, "that Dugléré served a banquet which will remain for all time a gastronomic classic."

"You are right," the Marquis agreed. "I have never eaten such food before or since."

"Then let's hope that he does his best for us this evening," the Vicomte de Casablanca said hopefully. "As our guest, Darleston, you must order what you fancy, but allow me to choose the wines."

"As you are my host, I will bow to your superior knowledge," the Marquis smiled.

By the time the food came the three men were deep in a Political discussion that lasted from the *hors d'oeuvres* to the dessert.

The Marquis had just finished a dish of *fromage de la Croix de Fer* when, as he bent across the table to make a point, he was conscious of someone standing beside him.

Before he could turn his head he heard a small breathless voice that he recognised say,

"P-please – can I – stay with you for a – moment – my Lord?"

He heard the fear in Linetta's voice before he saw her face and realised that she was in fact very frightened, more frightened indeed than she had been when she had come to his cabin on the Steamship.

Slowly he rose to his feet, noticing as he did so the ultra-fashionable and expensive gown, the way that her hair was arranged and to his astonishment the faint signs of red lip salve on her mouth.

This had been a last minute thought on the part of Blanche before they had left for the theatre.

Linetta had gone to her room to show her the new gown that had come from Madame Laferrière.

"Perfect!" Blanche had exclaimed. "The dress is simple, at the same time it has a *chic* that in my mind only Madame Laferrière can create."

"I am so glad you are pleased and do you like the way the *coiffeur* has done my hair?"

"Felix has great taste," Blanche nodded. "What he decrees today, all Paris follows tomorrow."

Linetta smiled, delighted that Blanche was satisfied. Then, just as she turned towards the door, Blanche stopped her.

"One moment, Linetta, come here."

She went to the dressing table picked up a small round box and said,

"With your marvellous complexion you need very few cosmetics, but a touch of red on your lips will make all the difference to your appearance."

Linetta looked at her wide-eyed.

"Are you – sure I should – use it?" she asked. "I always understood that women who painted their faces were – "

She stopped suddenly realising that what she had been about to say would sound rude.

Mademoiselle had spoken of actresses as being 'fast' and Linetta had the idea that what she had disapproved of in particular was that they used rouge and powder.

As if she knew what she had been about to say, Blanche smiled disarmingly and answered,

"All *cocottes,* my dear Linetta, have red lips. It is a decoration that they wear as proudly as a Frenchman sports the *Légion d'Honneur.*"

She applied the lip salve to Linetta's mouth.

It had not been in the least garish, but Linetta had been very conscious of it until she reached the theatre and then forgot all about it.

Even though much of the salve had been smudged away during dinner, there was still an outline of red on her soft lips and the Marquis looked at it now incredulously.

But it was the fear in Linetta's eyes that riveted his attention.

She glanced back over her shoulder at the entrance to the restaurant.

"Th-there is a – man," she stammered.

The Marquis smiled.

"Another one? Then we must do something about him."

He turned to his two friends, who had also stood up.

"If you will excuse me, I will take this lady home."

He turned from the table without introducing Linetta and guided her back through the crowded restaurant with his hand under her elbow.

He was well aware, as they reached the entresol, that she looked up nervously at one of the staircases, but he drew her onto the step outside and called for the Duc's carriage.

It was waiting in the square and, when the Marquis had helped Linetta into it, he gave the address of a small restaurant that was only a few streets away.

Then he jumped in beside her and the footman closed the door behind them.

"I am – sorry," Linetta said, "I should not have – taken you away from your friends, but I – did not – know what else to do."

"You knew I was there?" the Marquis asked.

"I – saw you when we – arrived," Linetta said, "but we – dined upstairs in a room – alone."

There was something in the way she said the last word that told the Marquis only too clearly what had happened.

"You are quite safe now," he tried to reassure her soothingly. "I am taking you somewhere quiet where we can talk. There are so many things I want to learn about you, Linetta."

He knew as he spoke that he had become increasingly curious about her ever since learning from his valet that she had left the *Gare du Nord* before he could be of any further assistance.

How, the Marquis asked now, could she have transformed herself so swiftly from the soberly dressed girl he had seen on the Steamship to the fashionable figure that now sat beside him?

And how was it possible that she should have red lips?

They reached their destination so quickly that there was no chance to say anything more.

The Marquis helped Linetta out, told the carriage to return to the *Café Anglais* and led her into one of the small, intimate little restaurants that are peculiar to Paris.

There were only two other couples seated on the comfortable sofas and the Marquis chose a table that was well away from them and where there was no possibility of their being overheard.

As they had both dined already, he ordered coffee and a bottle of champagne and then turned sideways to look at Linetta.

She was lovely, he thought, even lovelier than he remembered, but her eyes were just the same young, innocent and very frightened.

Then she said impulsively,

"I am so – glad you were – there! I knew you would – protect me."

"Why were you dining alone?" the Marquis asked. "Surely the people you are staying with should not have allowed it?"

"Was it – wrong?" Linetta asked. "But I did not really have – any choice."

"Suppose we start at the beginning?" the Marquis suggested. "When we talked on the Steamer, you told me that your friends would be meeting you at the *Gare du Nord*."

"I-I did not actually say so," Linetta replied. "As a matter of fact no one knew I was – coming to Paris. I had a letter of introduction to the – niece of my old Governess."

"What is her name?" the Marquis asked casually.

"Blanche d'Antigny," Linetta answered and did not notice that he stiffened in astonishment.

"Did you say *Blanche d'Antigny*?" he asked sharply.

"Yes," Linetta answered. "My Governess thought that her niece had employment – with a family in the *Rue de Friedland*, but it is her own house."

For the moment the Marquis was too astonished to speak.

He knew all about Blanche d'Antigny. It would have been impossible for him to move about Paris without doing so.

He had actually been a friend of the Prince she had gone to Russia with and before they left he had met Blanche on various occasions.

He had heard that she had returned to Paris and he knew that Raphael Bischoffsheim was her official lover. He was also been acquainted with a great number of other men who had been enraptured by Blanche at one time or another.

He could hardly take in the fact that Linetta was living with one of the most notorious *Demi-Mondaines* in Paris.

Skilfully he extracted from her the story of her life before she left England.

She told him about the quiet existence that she and her mother had lived in their small village. She described the affection she had for Mademoiselle Antigny, how there had been nothing left of her savings and how she had told her to go to France to her niece Marie-Ernestine.

"And Blanche d'Antigny has given you the clothes you are now wearing?" the Marquis asked.

Linetta nodded and then she blushed.

"I am afraid – Mr. Bischoffsheim has paid for them," she said shyly. "I did not think it – right that he should do so, but Blanche claimed that it was a present to her and anyway she could not take me about with her – looking as I did."

"Have you thought about the future?" the Marquis asked.

There was an obvious pause before Linetta said,

"Yes, my Lord – Blanche and a friend of hers – Madame Marguerite Bellanger – discussed it this – morning."

"And what did they decide?"

Linetta found it difficult to tell him. The question as to whether or not she should become a *Grande Cocotte* had worried her all day.

Marguerite Bellanger had explained it very plausibly and what she had said seemed at the time eminently sensible. Yet, now that she had to tell the Marquis what had been planned, she felt that he would think it odd.

Would he understand, being English, that as Marguerite had said, there was no alternative for her in France but to become a man's 'second wife'?

She had the feeling the Marquis that might be shocked.

Then she told herself that after all it was none of his business.

He had been kind to her, he had protected her not once but twice from the unwelcome attentions of strange men, but that did not give him the right to interfere in any decision she might make for herself.

But was it true that she had made such a decision?

She was not yet certain that she would do what Blanche and Marguerite expected of her. At the same time it was impossible to think of leaving the *Avenue de Friedland* and being alone in Paris.

She raised her eyes to look at the Marquis and he thought, as he had done before, that she looked not only very young but also pathetically innocent.

"Tell me," he asked quietly, "what have they suggested for you?"

"They – want me," Linetta answered in a voice that was hardly above a whisper, "to be – like them – a *Grande Cocotte.*"

CHAPTER FIVE

There was a long silence.

Then the Marquis enquired as if he deliberately changed the subject,

"Who frightened you?"

He saw Linetta's fingers tremble before she answered,

"When we were at the theatre tonight a – friend of Mr. Bischoffsheim came and sat in the box. He asked me out to dinner and I did not – realise that I had accepted his invitation until it was too – late to refuse."

"Who is he?" the Marquis enquired.

"Mr. Vossin – he is a Banker."

"I have heard of him."

The Marquis actually knew that Jacques Vossin was not only a Banker of some repute but also a man who had financial interests all over the world.

He could understand that Blanche, and certainly Mr. Bischoffsheim, would think it an honour and an opportunity for Linetta that he should wish to entertain her.

As the Marquis did not speak, Linetta went on after a moment,

"He seemed – old and – dull and it was only when dinner was – finished that he – behaved in a very – strange way."

"What did he do?" the Marquis enquired.

"He – tried to – kiss me!"

The blood rose in her face in a crimson tide.

"It was horrible! Horrible and very – frightening. He said that he was going to – catch me and I could not – escape from him. That is – why I came to – *you*."

"You did exactly the right thing."

The Marquis realised that she was not far from tears and he signalled to the waiter to pour out the champagne that was beside their table in an ice bucket.

"I can quite understand why you felt upset, Linetta, drink a little champagne, it will do you good."

Obediently Linetta raised the glass to her lips and after a moment the Marquis continued,

"When we met on the Steamship, had you any idea what you could do to earn money? You could not have expected Marie-Ernestine d'Antigny, who you thought was working for her living, to support you."

"No, of course, not," Linetta answered. "I imagined that I might teach – English to French children."

She paused to look up at the Marquis.

"But Blanche tells me that no lady would employ me. She said I am too young and too – pretty."

Linetta thought that this sounded conceited and again the colour rose in her face as she looked down, her eyelashes dark against her cheeks.

"That is certainly true!" the Marquis said dryly. "Is there nothing else you can do?"

Linetta made a helpless little gesture with her hands.

"I suppose, thanks to Mademoiselle Antigny, I am fairly well educated. I have read many books, I can sew, but I am afraid that I have no other qualifications."

The Marquis was silent and Linetta murmured pleadingly,

"Please, help me to decide what is – right. I was wishing only this morning that I could talk to you – and ask your advice."

"About the career that Blanche d'Antigny and Marguerite Bellanger have suggested for you?" he quizzed her.

"They explained to me that it is just like a man taking a – second wife, because in France his marriage is always one of *convenance,*" Linetta answered, "But I am not certain that Mama would have approved, even though she was French."

"I am quite certain that she would have disapproved most strongly!" the Marquis said positively.

Linetta looked at him with a startled expression in her eyes.

"I thought so too," she then admitted. "Although the way that Marguerite explained it sounded so – sensible. But the question is what else can I do?"

"There must be something," the Marquis said more to himself than to Linetta.

He realised that she was looking at him with an anxious expression on her face and after a moment he said,

"I think you must allow me a little time to think over this problem, so I suggest that we put it aside for the moment. I want you to tell me your impressions of Paris and, after you have finished your champagne, perhaps we could go for a drive. I don't suppose that anyone has yet shown you Paris by night."

Linetta's eyes lit up.

"I would love that," she answered, "and if you will not think it very rude, I don't want to drink any more. To be honest, I don't like champagne – very much."

"Then we will go now," the Marquis proposed.

He raised his hand and a waiter hurried forward to bring him the bill.

He put some notes down on the table and asked if the doorman would call a *voiture*.

"I want a good one," he insisted, "and the hood is to be open."

"*Oui, Monsieur*," the waiter replied and within a few moments he returned to announce that the carriage was at the door.

The Marquis helped Linetta to her feet and they went outside the restaurant to find quite a comfortable *voiture* with its hood open and its *cocher* waiting for instructions.

"Drive to the *Place de la Concorde*," the Marquis ordered as he joined Linetta on the back seat.

The white swansdown of her wrap framed the rounded column of her neck and, as she turned to look around her, it showed the exquisite line of her chin.

The Marquis noted the fashionable curls at the back of her hair and the small bunches of snowdrops.

'She looks like spring itself,' he thought and wondered how long it would be before Paris spoilt her and she grew hard and avaricious like all the other *Demi-Mondaines*.

'It must not happen,' he told himself and then wondered how he could prevent it.

They drove along the *Rue de Rivoli* and the Marquis told Linetta stories of the Tuilleries Gardens, which lay on their left.

When they reached the *Place de la Concorde*, it was brilliant with gaslight and they could see the fountains, the obelisk in the centre and the *Champs-Élysées* like a river of light as it led the eye upwards towards the starlit sky.

"It's so – beautiful!" Linetta exclaimed. "More beautiful than I imagined anything could be."

"Paris is at its best at this time of night," the Marquis told her, "when there is not so much traffic and very few people."

She gave him a little smile as if she thought the same. Then he instructed the *cocher* to stop on the other side of the fountains at the foot of the *Champs-Élysées*.

"The chestnuts are coming into bloom," he commented. "If we keep the *voiture*, would you like to walk a little way?"

"I would love it!" Linetta cried.

She knew that she would have agreed to anything he asked, because she was so afraid that he would take her home and her time with him would come to an end.

She had been so desperately frightened when Mr. Vossin had tried to kiss her and it had been an indescribable relief to find the Marquis and to be sure that he would protect her.

When she first spoke to him, she had been half-afraid that he would find her a nuisance and send her away. But, when he had taken her arm to guide her through the restaurant, she had felt her fears subsiding and had known that she really was safe.

To sit beside him, to listen to his deep voice and to know that he was thinking about her, made her feel as if all her troubles and difficulties had fallen from her shoulders and she was free and untrammelled simply because he was here.

'We must walk for a long way,' Linetta told herself as she climbed out of the carriage. 'I cannot go back to the *Avenue de Friedland* to lie awake wondering if I will ever see him again.'

Then she thought that perhaps Mr. Bischolfsheim and Blanche might be angry with her for having been rude to their friend, Mr. Vossin.

She was quite certain that Blanche would think it foolish and very childish of her to have been so afraid.

Could she not have refused his advances without running away after he had given her dinner?

But even to think of Mr. Vossin was to see his thin cadaverous face close to hers and she had known that there was an expression in his eyes that, while she did not understand it, made her want to scream.

She had felt the strength of his arm around her waist pulling her to him and she had known that she felt a repugnance for him that was the same as she had felt for the man in the plaid cape on the Steamship.

Why should such men terrify her? She could not explain it, she only knew that they did.

The gas globes every few yards along the avenue cast a golden glow on the pavement and it was easy by their light to see that pink and white chestnuts were in bloom and their blossoms were like Christmas candles above their heads.

Linetta looked up and the Marquis watched the perfect line of her neck and saw her small nose silhouetted against the darkness of the trees.

"It all seems enchanted," she exclaimed. "But then I am sure that Paris is an enchanted City."

"What makes you think that?" the Marquis enquired.

"I think it is because everyone talks about Paris almost in bated breath and always as if it was a woman. They never refer to London as 'she', but Paris is invariably feminine."

The Marquis laughed.

"That is true and she is at the moment the gayest, most entertaining and extravagant Capital in Europe."

"But there is also a great deal of poverty."

"How do you know that?"

"I have seen some very poor and ragged people – when we have been travelling to the theatre," Linetta answered, "and, when I asked the maid who waits on me in Blanche's house how much the average working people earn, it was – very very little."

"How much?" the Marquis asked her.

He was surprised that Linetta should have been interested to find out about the poor of Paris.

He was well aware that many of them lived in lamentable conditions and that behind the broad boulevards and the fine mansions built by Haussmann there were tumbledown insanitary shacks that were more squalid than anything that he had ever seen in England.

"The maid told me," Linetta replied in her gentle voice, "that the vast majority of women working in Paris live by needlework."

She paused, looked up at the Marquis and added,

"I did think at first that perhaps that was a way I could earn money, but I know I cannot embroider half as well as the Frenchwomen do."

"What are their wages?" the Marquis enquired.

"A very experienced needlewoman can earn perhaps – five francs a day," Linetta answered, "but most women get two."

She gave a deep sigh.

"How can they live on two francs a day?" she asked. "It seems in contrast very wrong that a gown from Monsieur Worth costs one thousand two hundred francs."

The Marquis knew that she was speaking the truth, but he thought it unlikely that Blanche or any of her kind worried as to how much the sewing women who made their gowns were paid, as long as there was a man to meet the bills when they were presented.

They walked on a little way and then the Marquis slipped Linetta's arm through his and put his other hand over hers.

"You are the immediate problem," he declared. "So before you start worrying about the poor of Paris, think about yourself."

"I am likely to become – one of them," Linetta replied.

"I think that is improbable," the Marquis answered and he was thinking of Jacques Vossin as he spoke.

He was well aware how easy it would be for Linetta with the help of Blanche and Marguerite to meet all the richest and most important men of Paris.

Every night they attended one of the parties given by the *Demi-Mondaines* and anyone as young, fresh, and unspoilt as Linetta would immediately attract their attention.

The Marquis had not missed Linetta's reference to being a 'second wife'. It was a plausible description.

At the same time the Marquis wondered if she had any idea how short-lived the majority of such pretence marriages turned out to be.

There were exceptions, of course. Blanche had remained with her Prince for nearly five years, but then they had been in Russia.

Cora Pearl had been under the protection of the Duc de Mornay for several years, but she had certainly not been faithful to him and she had a necklace that was a record of her changing heart.

It was a massive gold chain hung with twelve lockets each containing a portrait. Of the most exquisite workmanship each locket was emblazoned with the arms of an ancient family of France.

Was that the future for Linetta? The Marquis could not bear to think of it.

'I will find her something else,' he told himself.

Then because they had now walked quite a distance up the avenue he suggested,

"I think we should go back."

'He is taking me home,' Linetta thought, 'and then perhaps I will never see him again.'

To delay the time she stepped off the pavement and onto the grass at the side of it.

The trunks of the chestnut trees stood like sentinels and it was very quiet beneath their branches now that the birds had gone to sleep.

She walked forward and the Marquis followed her.

"We might be in the country," she exclaimed. "How clever to have so many trees in the very centre of Paris."

"It was well planned," the Marquis replied rather absent-mindedly, as if he was thinking of something else.

Linetta moved on and then she stopped and looked back.

Her fair hair and white gown caught the distant lights, but she appeared waif-like and insubstantial in the semi-darkness.

She looked up at the Marquis and saw that his eyes were on her face.

"What are you – thinking?" she asked.

"I was thinking about you."

There was a note in his voice that made a little tremor of excitement run through her. Then it seemed as if neither of them could move, they could only stand there gazing at each other.

"What am I to do about you, Linetta?" the Marquis asked after a moment.

"Could I – could I not – stay with you?"

Her voice was very low and yet he could hear every word.

Then, as he was still, she moved towards him. It was instinctive as a flower turns towards the sun or as something small and frightened seeks safety and security.

Almost automatically his arms went round her.

"I am not – afraid when you are – here," she whispered.

She turned up her face as she spoke, trying to see the expression in his.

Then, almost without intending to do so, his lips were on hers.

Her mouth was very soft and he was very gentle.

It was a kiss without passion, a kiss that a man might give to a child, until, as their lips were joined together, something strange and wonderful seemed to rise within them both.

The Marquis held Linetta closer to him and his lips became more demanding.

To Linetta the whole world was suffused with a golden light and she felt a thrill like quicksilver run through her, giving her a sublime sensation that she had never known or even imagined before in her life.

It was as if she came alive and her whole body vibrated to the wonder of it, yet at the same time she could no longer think objectively and she was no longer herself.

She had ceased to exist and had become a part of the Marquis.

His mouth held her captive and, while her whole self merged with his, she knew with a wild inexplicable ecstasy that this was love!

She had not expected it, she had not even sought it and yet it was here, love, so that she gave herself to him and her heart and soul became his.

The Marquis raised his head.

"My sweet! My darling!" he exclaimed. "I did not mean this to happen."

"I *love* – you!" Linetta whispered. "I did not – know that was why I wanted to be with – you – but I love – you!"

She spoke in the faraway bemused voice of someone who has just woken from a dream.

In the light from a distant gas-globe the Marquis could see that her face was radiant.

His lips sought hers again and now, as he felt her respond and knew that he had for the first time awakened in her a tiny flame in answer to the fire that was rising inside him, his lips became more insistent.

He knew that she was not afraid and he knew too that her lips had brought him a magic that he had never experienced before.

There had been a great many women in the Marquis's life, but all of them had been experienced sophisticates, who had wanted him almost before he was aware that he was attracted to them, women who had used every trick and artifice of femininity to get what they wanted.

He thought, as he kissed, Linetta that it was an experience he had never known to touch lips that were innocent and to awaken a girl to womanhood who had never known love.

When he took his mouth from hers, Linetta hid her face against his shoulder as if the passion that she had aroused in him and in herself made her shy.

Even as she did so the Marquis felt that she was trembling and it was not from fear.

He drew in a deep breath.

"What has happened to us, Linetta?"

"We are – enchanted. I told you – this was an – enchanted place."

"You were right! And it is an enchantment that I have never known before."

She raised her head from his shoulder.

"Is that – true?" she questioned. "You must have seen so much of the world and known so many – women. I am ignorant and – inexperienced because I have never met a man like you before."

"I realise that, Linetta, and that is why I must look after you."

"That is what I want you to do," she replied. "Could I – could I be your – *chère amie?*"

She thought for one frightening moment that he was going to refuse, although he did not move it was almost as if he drew away from her.

Then he said in a disjointed voice,

"Is that what you really want? Are you asking me to be your protector?"

"I want to be with – you. I want you to – protect me."

She paused to add,

"I have wanted that ever since I first – saw you and now I know I love – you."

"I thought it was impossible for anyone to fall in love at first sight," the Marquis said, "but I was wrong!"

She waited a little apprehensively and he finished,

"After we had met on the Steamship, I found myself thinking about you incessantly. I could not understand why you kept coming into my thoughts."

Linetta drew in a deep breath of happiness.

"Perhaps we were – meant for each – other," she sighed. "Perhaps it was Fate that brought me to your cabin – that made me know that you could – help me."

"And it was Fate that we met again tonight," the Marquis pointed out. "I wished over and over again after I had lost you that I had asked you where you were going."

As he spoke, he wondered whether if Linetta had told him at Calais that she was staying with Blanche d'Antigny, he would have tried to dissuade her.

Now he knew that he could not allow her to remain in the *Avenue de Friedland*.

Because he was not certain what he should say to her about it, he kissed her again.

As he felt her quiver against him, he felt that he was transported by a strange magic that he could truthfully say he had never known in his life before.

One small critical part of his mind told him it was impossible that he, who was usually so cynical, could feel like a boy infatuated by his first love affair.

And yet it was true.

He had not known it was possible to feel as if Linetta was not a human being but a figment of his dreams and that she brought him all the ideals of Chivalry, the legends of mythology and the aspirations of heroism that he had forgotten as he had grown older.

Finally as they drew apart, the Marquis felt as if his own face was as radiant as Linetta's and that his eyes too shone with a light that had something spiritual about it.

Without speaking Linetta slipped her hand into his and they walked back through the trees to the *Place de la Concorde* where the carriage was waiting for them.

Still in silence the Marquis helped Linetta in.

Then, as the horses moved off, she turned towards him with an inarticulate little murmur and put her face against his shoulder.

"Are you happy, my precious?" he asked.

"So unbelievably – marvellously – happy," she answered. "I feel as if my whole body is singing with the joy of knowing you and because you – kissed me."

The Marquis lifted her hand to his lips.

"You are mine!"

"That is what I want to be," Linetta murmured. "When can I be with – you?"

"We will talk it over tomorrow," the Marquis answered. "I want to take you away from that house and I will find somewhere where we can be together."

He saw the expression on Linetta's face and knew how happy it made her.

"What shall I tell Blanche?" she asked. "Perhaps she will be – angry with me because I was – rude tonight in running away from – Mr. Vossin."

"I will call and talk to Blanche d'Antigny tomorrow," the Marquis told her. "What time is she awake?"

"Not very early," Linetta replied. "But I expect she will go to a rehearsal at about eleven o'clock."

"I will call at half-past ten," the Marquis decided. 'Will you leave a message with the maid or shall I tell the footman?"

"I will tell the maid when she brings my breakfast."

She paused and there was a worried note in her voice as she added,

"You will – come? You will not – change your mind?"

"You know you can trust me."

"I am not being a nuisance – or an – encumbrance? You know I would not wish to be."

"I think we both know that what we feel for each other is something very different from what we might be expected to think or feel," the Marquis answered. "We have not known each other long, Linetta, and yet you say that you love me and I do *not* believe that it is entirely due to the magic of the night or the lights in the *Champs-Élysées*."

"No, no – it is not that," Linetta said quickly. "It's because I feel that I actually belong to you – that I have always – belonged to you."

She paused and then continued,

"It's difficult to – explain but the feeling is – there."

"It is a feeling that is true," the Marquis replied. "As I have already said, Linetta, you are mine and, although I have a few plans to make, I promise you that by this time tomorrow night I will tell you what they are."

"Thank you! *Thank you!*"

"When you get back you are to go to sleep. You are not to worry about anything. Leave everything to me."

"That is what I want to do," Linetta said. "Equally I cannot help feeling that I have – thrust myself upon – you."

"Have we not just said that it was Fate?" he asked. "And Fate is something that neither of us can control."

"I have no wish to – change mine."

She put her head once again against the Marquis's shoulder and it was a caress.

"I was so worried all day," she confessed. "I thought that what Marguerite had suggested to me was deeply wrong and that Mama would – disapprove, but now I am no longer afraid or apprehensive,"

"And you think that your mother would approve of what we intend to do?" the Marquis enquired.

Linetta considered the question for a moment and then she said,

"I am sure that Mama would understand. And because she loved my father as I love you, she would be glad that I am so happy."

The Marquis did not answer and, as the carriage drew up outside number 11 *Avenue de Friedland,* Linetta lifted her head to look a little nervously towards the front door.

"Go straight to bed, my darling," the Marquis urged her. "If Blanche is at home, which I doubt since it is still fairly early by Parisian standards, don't tell her what happened tonight. Leave me to talk to her tomorrow."

"I want to do that," Linetta answered.

He lifted first one of her hands to his lips and then the other.

"I shall be thinking of – you," he sighed gently.

"I could think of no one else," Linetta replied, "and I shall be counting the minutes until tomorrow when I can see you again."

"We will have luncheon together. After I have seen Blanche I will ask for you."

"I will be – waiting."

The Marquis stepped from the carriage to help Linetta onto the pavement, they walked up the steps and he rang the bell.

They heard the night porter coming towards the door and Linetta looked up.

"You will not – forget that I love – you?" she asked the Marquis in a whisper.

"It would be impossible for me to do so," he answered gravely.

As the door opened, he kissed her hand and walked back to the waiting *voiture.*

*

The following morning Linetta awoke with a feeling of excitement and happiness that she had not known since she had been a child on Christmas morning.

For a moment she was too sleepy to remember why she should feel so rapturous until the memory of the night before swept over her like a shaft of sunlight.

Then, as she closed her eyes again, she could feel the Marquis's arms around her and his lips on hers.

She had never realised that a kiss could make her feel as if the world was left behind and she was swept up into the sky.

She could feel herself vibrate to the touch of the Marquis's mouth, to his arms holding her and to the note in his deep voice that made her feel shy.

'I love him and love is more wonderful and more marvellous than I had any idea it could be,' Linetta told herself.

She could understand for the first time why her mother had found it impossible to talk about her father without crying.

She knew now that if she lost the Marquis her whole world would fall apart and there would be nothing left but an impenetrable darkness.

She wished that she had understood how deeply her mother had mourned the man she loved. She remembered how her mother had often sat in the garden gazing at the flowers and yet, Linetta was sure, seeing nothing but her husband who had died and her youth, which had died with him.

'I did not understand,' she whispered.

But now she knew that love was something that permeated her whole being and without love there was only a barren desert of emptiness.

'I must never lose him,' Linetta told herself.

She felt herself thrill when she recalled that he had said that she no longer need worry about the future and that he would look after her.

'We will be together,' she thought and wondered if he was thinking of her in the same way that she was thinking of him.

When the maid brought her *petit déjeuner*, she asked her to tell Blanche as soon as she awoke that the Marquis of Darleston was calling on her at half-past ten,

"I'll tell Madame, if she's awake before then," the maid replied,

"Surely she is going to rehearsal this morning?" Linetta asked.

The maid shrugged her shoulders.

"Maybe she is and maybe she isn't. I understand it was five o'clock this mornin' before Madame got home from the party. She'll need her sleep."

"Yes, she will indeed," Linetta agreed.

At the same time she felt worried in case Blanche would not be awake to see the Marquis when he called.

"Well, anyway, Madame can sleep tonight," the maid went on as she tidied Linetta's clothes and put away the shoes that she had worn the night before.

"Why particularly?" Linetta asked.,

"Monsieur is going to the country," the maid replied. "I understand he has to be at the sixteenth birthday party of his eldest daughter."

Linetta sat up in bed.

"His daughter?" she asked.

"Monsieur has four children," the maid answered. "They are very spoilt accordin' to Jules, Monsieur's coachman. He says their mother indulges them and their father gives them too much money."

She gave a sharp laugh.

"I wish I could say the same about my father. The only money he ever has is what I give him and that's precious little out of my wages."

She went from the room and Linetta sat staring after her.

She did not know why but it perturbed her to think about Mr. Bischoffsheim's children.

She somehow supposed, after what Blanche and Marguerite had said, that he would have a wife. But children! What did they think about Blanche if they knew about her?

Perhaps they were kept discreetly in the country and had no idea what their father did when he was in Paris.

That would be the obvious arrangement, Linetta told herself. But then she thought that it must be difficult to keep them in ignorance when they were growing up.

Then she told herself severely that what Mr. Bischoffsheim did was no concern of hers. All that really mattered was that she should be with the Marquis and that he should kiss her again as he had done last night.

She found herself praying.

'Please, God, let him go on loving me. Please let us be happy together and help Mama to understand that there was nothing else I could do but agree to what Marguerite and Blanche suggested until I found the Marquis again.'

~130~

She ate her breakfast and then got up, choosing the prettiest of her new dresses, several of which had arrived the previous afternoon.

They were very different from the dark, unfashionable travelling gown that she had worn on the Steamship. And yet the Marquis said that he had found it impossible to forget her! So perhaps she had not looked as unattractive as she thought she had.

She watched the clock and more than once lifted it to her ear thinking that it must have stopped as time went by so slowly.

'I am going to see him again!'

It was like a psalm of joy and every time she said the words the sunshine seemed brighter as it shone through the window into her room.

Blanche had awoken at half-past ten to be told the Marquis of Darleston was downstairs waiting to see her.

She sat up in bed, asked the maid for a brush to tidy her hair with, applied a powder puff to her nose and a red salve to her lips.

"You may show him up," she said and patted the lace pillows into a pile behind her.

When the Marquis entered Blanche's bedroom, he looked at the fantastic blue and white bed and the transparent nightgown of its occupant.

Then his eyes twinkled.

"How delightful to see you again, my Lord!" Blanche exclaimed. "I was not expecting you to call on me."

"We met with His Highness," the Marquis replied, "and I heard of your sensational success in Russia."

Smiling and at his ease he walked to the side of the bed and, taking the hand that Blanche extended to him, raised it to his lips.

Then he seated himself in an armchair and his eyes were still amused.

"And even more of a sensation in Paris," Blanche added defiantly.

"I arrived only the day before yesterday," the Marquis said, "but I hope I shall have the pleasure of seeing you at the *Folies Dramatiques*."

Blanche gave him an enticing smile as he went on,

"But I have come to see you this morning about Linetta."

Blanche looked surprised.

"Linetta?" she exclaimed. "Where did you meet her?"

"We met on the cross-channel Steamer on our way to Paris," the Marquis told her. "Last night she was terrified by the man who was giving her dinner and very wisely she sought my protection."

"Jacques Vossin?" Blanche questioned. "How could he have been such a fool?"

The Marquis did not reply and she went on,

"He must have realised how innocent Linetta is. He should have approached her very carefully. If I had known that he was taking her out to dinner, I would have warned him."

"It is a pity you omitted to do so."

"It was all arranged while I was still on the stage," Blanche explained. "When Bisch told me where she had gone I thought then that it was a great mistake. At the same time Jacques is enormously rich and apparently, as he told

Bisch, he has taken a fancy to Linetta. She would want for nothing!"

"She dislikes him," the Marquis replied, "and to put it bluntly, I intend to take care of her myself."

Blanche raised her eyebrows.

"Why not? But are you staying in Paris long?"

This was a question that the Marquis had already asked himself.

"I am not certain of my plans, but you can be quite certain that whatever they may be, I shall look after Linetta."

Blanche looked at him speculatively.

"I can quite imagine that Linetta would find it difficult to resist your handsome face and what I have always been told is a most persuasive tongue. But you are English! Do you intend to take her back to England with you when you return home?"

The Marquis did not answer and Blanche went on,

"Perhaps she would be happy in one of those discreet little Villas in St. John's Wood. But when you are bored with her, send her back to Paris. I am quite convinced that she would be a sensation here. She looks so different from everyone else!"

"That is what I think," the Marquis said. "Equally may I compliment you, Blanche. You are even more beautiful than before you went to Russia."

"Thank you, kind sir," Blanche smiled.

"I shall be taking Linetta away as soon as I have found a house or an apartment," the Marquis said in what was almost a businesslike tone. "But before I do so, I would like to reimburse your friend Mr. Bischoffsheim for what he has spent on her."

"There is no need," Blanche replied. "Bisch can well afford it and the bills will not be a quarter of what I spend in a week!"

"I am sure of that," the Marquis responded. "At the same time I would rather pay for Linetta myself,"

"As you please," Blanche said lightly. "I will tell Madame Laferrière to send you her account and I believe Marguerite ordered a few gowns for her yesterday from Worth."

"The British Embassy will always find me," the Marquis informed her. "I collect my letters from there every other day."

He rose to his feet.

"I would like to thank you for looking after Linetta and I appreciate it that you did your best for her."

"I doubt if you really think it was the best," Blanche answered perceptively. "But then what else could she do? She is, as you well know, far too lovely to be alone in Paris. What choice did she have? There are men, *mon cher* Marquis, in every walk of life,"

"As you say, she is far too beautiful not to need protecting from the type of man who frightens her."

Blanche laughed.

"Poor Jacques! It must have been a shock for him to find one woman who is not interested in his many millions!"

"I daresay he will soon find adequate consolation," the Marquis remarked dryly as he kissed Blanche's hand.

"Thank you again, Blanche," he murmured.

"There is no need. And may I say, my Lord, that you are always a welcome guest in this house?"

The Marquis smiled but did not react.

When he had gone from the room, Blanche threw herself back against the pillows.

"What a man! What looks!" she exclaimed out loud. "Little Linetta is more astute than I gave her credit for!"

CHAPTER SIX

"Are you happy, my darling?"

The Marquis laid his hand on Linetta's as he spoke.

She smiled up at him, her eyes shining.

There was really no need for her to reply. It was so obvious that happiness radiated from her.

"Happier than I ever believed – it possible," she said in a low voice.

It had indeed been a day of enchantment.

After the Marquis had seen Blanche, he and Linetta had driven away to look at a place to rent that the Duc de Rochfort had recommended.

The Marquis had told him what he wanted and the Duc had said,

"Setting up house, Darleston? I don't blame you, I only had a glimpse of her, but she looks enchanting."

"She is," the Marquis answered briefly.

The Duc smiled.

"You are being very English, my friend. A Frenchman would go into ecstasies over a girl so exquisite. But I feel that you are genuinely captivated and I am indeed delighted."

"Why?" the Marquis enquired.

"Because I am too fond of you to see you fleeced by all the old hands at the game. However much we may think we can avoid their wiles, the Cora Pearls and the La Païvas of this world are far too astute at emptying a man's pockets for him to be able to circumvent them."

"I assure you that I am well able to take care of myself," the Marquis countered with a smile.

The Duc had, however, told him that a friend was leaving on the following day for North Africa.

"Henri is a connoisseur," he said. "His house is full of valuable furniture and old masterpieces. He would not let it to an ordinary person who would give rough parties and undoubtedly ruin the Aubusson carpets, but you are different."

"I would hope so," the Marquis replied.

"Anyway I will send him a note and ask if you can view the house this morning. I have a feeling that it will please you."

The Duc had been right. The house was, the Marquis thought, a perfect setting for Linetta.

It had been built in the last century and combined the taste and elegance of Louis XV with modern amenities.

Standing a little way from the *Champs-Élysées* it was surrounded by a small garden. The rooms were small and most of them were panelled.

There was no doubt its owner had perfect taste and he had collected over the years many *objets d'art* which, because they were unique, had an incalculable value.

There was an old family servant to show them round, who informed the Marquis that he and his wife were prepared to look after anyone who rented the house while his Master was away.

When he had taken them into every room, the old man withdrew and Linetta stood in the salon looking out onto the flower-filled garden.

"Do you like it?" the Marquis asked her.

"It's just perfect. Rather like a doll's house!" It is complete in every detail, but not too overwhelming to be frightening,"

"You will not be frightened here with me," the Marquis promised.

"I would not be frightened anywhere with – you and I know that we will be happy here."

"I know that too," he added.

Then, drawing her into his arms, he looked down at her face.

"You are so lovely and so unspoilt. I have a feeling really that I should take you away from Paris and find some uninhabited island where we should be entirely alone."

"I should like that," she said, "but I should be afraid that I might – bore you."

It was a real fear because Linetta was very conscious that to the Marquis she must seem very ignorant and juvenile.

Yet as the day progressed she found it was very easy to talk to him, in fact a joy that she had not expected. She had never had the opportunity of meeting men, let alone talking with one.

As they sat at luncheon in a quiet part of the *Bois de Boulogne* that was not fashionable, she found that there was so much he had to tell her and so much she wanted to learn.

The Marquis discovered that Linetta was not only well read but she also thought a great deal.

He had never expected to be alone with a woman and find himself interested and amused without flirting, or without fighting a duel of wits that centred entirely upon the fact that she was a woman and he a man.

Linetta spoke to him as if he possessed all the wisdom of the world and yet she was prepared to voice her own opinions. Which he found were not only original but sometimes provocative.

He found himself forgetting how young she was and talking to her as if she was an equal.

"There is so much we have to – discover about each – other," Linetta said a little shyly as the luncheon ended and the Marquis thought that it was just what he might have said himself.

"Everything I learn about you makes me surer than ever that you are different from any other woman I have ever met," he told her.

He saw the light come into her eyes at the compliment and then she said with a sudden change of tone,

"What will – happen to me if I – bore you?"

"That is something I am convinced will never happen."

"But it – might," she persisted.

"I think that we can leave anything so improbable and so utterly unlikely to the future," the Marquis said.

She looked away from him across the garden of the restaurant and he could see her profile silhouetted against the flowers.

"What is worrying you?" he asked softly.

"When I am with you," Linetta replied, "it is difficult to think clearly since I am so happy. It is like floating on a sunbeam and being so high above the world that its problems and difficulties are far away in the distance. But I somehow feel that I ought to face up to the future."

"Forget it," the Marquis responded to her briefly. "Let's only think of today and allow tomorrow to take care of itself."

He rose from the table as he spoke and put a large number of notes on the bill that was lying beside him. Then he took Linetta to where the carriage was waiting.

They had driven along the Seine since the Marquis wanted her to see the beauty of the new bridges spanning the silver water and the magnificent facade of *Notre-Dame*.

And she had returned to the *Avenue de Friedland* at about five o'clock.

She learnt that Blanche was resting, but had left a message that she wanted to see her so she went upstairs to her boudoir.

"There is no need for me to ask if you have enjoyed yourself," Blanche smiled, looking at her face.

"It has been a wonderful day," Linetta answered. "And we have found a charming house that we can move into tomorrow after luncheon. May I ask the maids to pack for me?"

"But, of course," Blanche answered, "and I suspect that I shall have to lend you some trunks. The one that you arrived with will hardly hold all your new acquisitions."

"Thank you!"

"His Lordship insists on paying for them. He obviously intends to start your liaison in the right way."

Linetta did not know what to say to this. She only wished that Marguerite had not insisted on spending so much money at Worth's.

As if she read her thoughts, Blanche said,

"He is generous for an Englishman and remember that a man wants to be proud of the woman who belongs to him. He wants her to look more beautiful and more elegant than any other woman he sees."

Linetta felt that she could never look as beautiful as Blanche with her golden hair and vivid blue eyes, her milk-white skin and voluptuous body!

To change the subject she said hesitatingly,

"You do not think it – rude of me to leave you like this after all your kindness? I am most deeply grateful, I am really."

"You have solved your own future in an extremely clever manner," Blanche told her. "I think the Marquis is delightful and very handsome!"

She paused and then added,

"I think I must do my duty, Linetta, by advising you to be sensible."

"Sensible?" Linetta enquired.

Blanche nodded.

"Love does not last for ever, but jewels do! They are an essential insurance against the future."

"I don't – think I – understand," Linetta faltered.

"I will show you something."

Blanche pointed to the Boule writing desk in the corner of the boudoir.

"Open the desk," she suggested. "I was using it this morning, so the key is in the lock. And bring me the case you find inside."

Wonderingly Linetta obeyed her.

Inside the desk she found not writing materials as she might have expected, but a large leather-covered jewel case, which was surprisingly heavy as she carried it across the room.

Blanche sat up on the *chaise-longue* and put the case on her knee.

She opened it and Linetta gave a little gasp.

Inside there was a profusion of jewels such as she had never imagined could all be accumulated in one place.

There were necklaces, earrings, brooches and bracelets, rings and lockets, all sparkling and glittering so that they seemed almost to be alive.

Linetta looked at them with a bemused expression on her face.

"Are – all these jewels – yours?"

"They are all mine," Blanche answered. "And you will understand, Linetta, when I tell you that whatever happens to me they will remain the most permanent and lasting *cher ami* of them all."

"I could not – expect the Marquis to give me – anything like that," Linetta protested.

"You not only have to expect it, you have to ask, you have to insist!" Blanche said. "Every woman, make no mistake about this, Linetta, who gives her favours to a man should see that he provides her with somewhere to live, with beautiful clothes that she will be admired in and splendid jewels."

She paused for a moment to add,

"She is also entitled to lackeys, carriages, a chef and these must all be paid for by her protector. The man who proclaims to the world that he has won her favour *must* give her a tangible proof of his affection."

"She is so thin and the baby is ill," she said almost as if she was speaking to herself.

"There is nothing you can do about it," the Marquis told her. "And at least she will have enough food for a day or two."

"It was very kind of you, but it seems wrong that she should suffer without there being anywhere she can go to for help."

The Marquis did not reply, but when he had gone and Linetta was going up the stairs to see Blanche she noted that there were several great baskets of flowers standing in the hall that must have been delivered during the afternoon.

One was of purple orchids and Linetta knew how very expensive they were.

When she was dressing, she could not help thinking of Blanche's fabulous jewels and the woman and baby who had been starving outside the house.

It was difficult too not to think of the dinner that Blanche had given, which had included peacock, the choice wines that had succeeded each other with every course, the table which had been laden with gold and silver ornaments and the women in their elaborate spectacular gowns, each of which had cost a fortune.

'Why does the Emperor not do something?' Linetta wondered and thought that she must ask the Marquis for an explanation.

But when she saw the Marquis again and knew that he admired her in her green gown she found it difficult to think of anything but him.

He had taken her to a restaurant that was not as large or as smart as the *Café Anglais*, but was yet, he told her, one of the very best in Paris.

The *Grand Véfour* was, in the *Palais Royal* and had been there, Linetta learnt, before the Revolution.

"I am going to order you their great speciality," the Marquis promised.

They had seated themselves on a red sofa in a small square room where the panels on the wall were beautifully painted with flowers and fruit.

"What is it?" Linetta enquired.

"It is a Rhenish carp," he replied, "a fish you will certainly not find in England. It is boned and stuffed, surrounded by soft roes and a hundred ingredients that only the *Grand Véfour* knows the secret of."

When the dish came, Linetta very much enjoyed it, but it was difficult to concentrate on what she was eating for she wanted only to talk to the Marquis, to listen to him and to ask him dozens of the questions that she felt only he could have an answer for.

He was very gay tonight, he made her laugh and they talked for so long that there was no time left to go to the theatre as he had planned.

He had not wished to take her to see Blanche but to one of the famous dramatic theatres in Paris where she could have seen Sarah Bernhardt or one of the other great actresses or actors who the Parisians were so proud of.

Instead they went on talking, finding what they had to say to each other far more intriguing than anything they might have seen performed on a stage.

Afterwards they drove, as they had done the night before, along the gas-lit streets under the stars to look at Paris in all its beauty, to see the Seine moving beneath its high banks and to find, as many people had found before them, that Paris is a City for lovers.

"You are so sweet, so adorable," the Marquis said with his arm round Linetta as they drove down streets where the only sound was the clop-clop of their horses' hoofs.

"I want to please you," she answered him simply.

"There are no words in English, or in French for that matter, to tell you how much you delight me," the Marquis went on. "Never before have I found myself listening to every note and intonation in a woman's voice. Everything you say, my darling, has a magic all of its own."

Linetta drew a deep breath.

"When you say things to me like that, it hurts me because it is so wonderful."

The Marquis drew her a little closer.

"I know exactly what you are trying to say, because I feel the same. I think you must be a Siren! You have bewitched me and I can no longer think of anything but you."

She lifted her face to his and he kissed her gently. But when she would have clung closer to him, he raised his head, releasing her lips to kiss her hair.

"Tomorrow night," he said in his deep voice, "we shall be alone in our little house, then I can show you, my precious, how much you mean to me and I can kiss you properly, as I want to do now."

Linetta felt herself thrill to the passion in his voice.

"It will be wonderful to be alone with you," she replied, "and to know that we shall not have to leave each other.

Last night when you had gone I wanted to run after you and tell you to come back. I was so afraid I might not see you again."

"Do you really think that could happen?" the Marquis asked. "I have already told you, Linetta, you are mine and we can never escape from each other."

"That is what I want to believe," she sighed, "but sometimes I am afraid."

"There is no reason to be. I will come for you early tomorrow morning. When I signed the lease this evening, I learnt that the owner of our house is leaving very early. We can therefore move in before noon if that pleases you."

"You know that nothing could be more wonderful!" Linetta cried.

Then the Marquis told her,

"Afterwards I must take you to Oscar Massin's and buy you a present. I meant to choose you something today, but we never seemed to have a moment. I was wondering which jewel would become you best, my precious."

He felt Linetta stiffen in his arms.

"I don't – want you to buy me – any jewellery," she stammered after a moment.

"Why not?" the Marquis asked in surprise.

She paused and he had the distinct feeling that she was trying to find an explanation other than the real one.

"You have given me – so much already," she said. "Blanche told me that you are – paying for my gowns."

"You don't suppose I would allow any other man to pay for them?" the Marquis asked. "But I want to give you many things, Linetta, and jewellery is only one of them."

"Please – I would rather not have it."

He put his hand under her chin and turned her face around so that he could look down into her eyes.

"Why?" he asked. "Tell me why?"

For a moment she tried to refuse him and then the masterful note in his voice made her obey him.

"This – evening Blanche showed me her – jewels," she stuttered.

The Marquis gave a little laugh.

"I understand what you are thinking, but I promise you it will not be the same."

He felt that she was not convinced and after a moment he declared,

"I would not do anything to upset you. Such things can wait. All that matters for the moment is that we should be together."

"Yes, that is the only thing that is of – any importance," Linetta agreed eagerly and lifted her lips to his.

They drove back to the *Avenue de Friedland* and, as the horses neared Blanche's house, the Marquis kissed Linetta's hands, his lips lingering on each of her small fingers and then her soft palm.

"Tomorrow night, my precious. I will kiss you as I want to do now. Till then we will be apart only for a few hours, although it will seem like a century to me."

"And to – me," Linetta replied.

The coachman drew the horses to a standstill and they stepped out onto the pavement.

"Sleep well, my darling, and dream of me," the Marquis suggested.

Linetta entered the house and the night footman closed the door behind her.

"Is Madame home yet?" Linetta asked him.

"Yes, *m'mselle*," the footman replied, "but I don't think she wishes to be disturbed."

"No, of course not," Linetta agreed. "I will be very quiet. Goodnight, Jules."

"Goodnight, *m'mselle*."

The footman crossed the hall and disappeared under the stairs through a door that led to the basement as Linetta started to walk up the staircase.

She was halfway up when she heard a tap at the front door.

She thought at once that it must be the Marquis who had forgotten something and, without waiting for the footman to return, she ran back down the stairs and opened the door herself.

Outside on the doorstep was not the Marquis but Mr. Bischoffsheim with a parcel in his hand.

"Mr. Bischoffsheim!" Linetta exclaimed in surprise. "I thought you were in the country."

He smiled at her and entered the hall to put his top hat down on a table.

"I was, but I came back to Paris because the only birthday present my daughter wanted was to be taken to the theatre."

He gave a little chuckle and added,

"She has her father's predilection for the footlights and wanted to see Madame Sarah Bernhardt in *Le Passant*."

"Was she very good?" Linetta asked.

"Magnificent!" Mr. Bischoffsheim exclaimed.

He looked at Linetta's gown and the wrap round her shoulders.

"Have you just come in?" he enquired.

"Just this moment and Blanche is back, but I think she is asleep."

"Then I am going to surprise her," Mr. Bischoffsheim said.

"I have a very special present here, one that she has wanted for a long time. Would you like to see it?"

"Yes, of course," Linetta answered.

Mr. Bischoffsheim glanced at his carriage footman who had brought in a basket of tuberoses, its handle trimmed with blue ribbons. He set it down in the hall.

"Is that all, *monsieur*?" he enquired.

"Yes, thank you, Clement," Mr. Bischoffsheim replied, "and be round at the usual time in the morning. Goodnight."

"Goodnight, *monsieur*," the footman answered and left the house closing the door behind him.

Linetta looked surprised.

She had not realised since coming to live with Blanche that Mr. Bischoffsheim ever stayed the night.

She thought it rather odd, but she naturally could not comment on it and he was concerned for the moment with opening the box that he was holding in his hands.

Linetta saw that it was covered in black velvet and she guessed before he raised the lid that it contained jewellery.

When he showed it to her, she gave a little gasp of sheer astonishment.

Never had she imagined that a necklace could be so magnificent, so encrusted with huge diamonds or flash more vividly in the dim lights of the hall.

"Do you like it?" Mr. Bischoffsheim asked.

"It's fantastic!" Linetta exclaimed.

"It belonged to Marie Antoinette," he explained, "and Blanche has coveted it for a long time. I had to do a great deal of hard bargaining, but now it is hers. Do you think she will be pleased?"

"How could she be anything else?"

Linetta wondered as she spoke why Blanche wanted more diamonds when she already had a huge boxful of them in her writing bureau.

"Come along," Mr. Bischoffsheim said, "we will surprise her. Do you think you can carry the flowers for me?"

"Yes, of course," Linetta answered.

She picked up the basket finding that it was lighter than it looked, and Mr. Bischoffsheim went ahead of her up the stairs.

As they reached the landing, he put a finger to his lips and they both walked very softly to Blanche's door.

He turned the handle gently and entered the room.

Linetta had expected it to be in darkness, but she saw that there was a candelabrum with two lit candles on the furthest side of the bed behind the blue and white silk curtains.

There was the fragrance of perfume and flowers as she followed Mr. Bischoffsheim into the room.

Then, as he reached the bed, he made a sound that was half a shout and half a cry.

It seemed to reverberate round the walls. Linetta, just a few steps inside the door, stiffened into immobility.

She saw Blanche stir and move her head from the pillow where her hair fell like a golden cloud.

Then incredibly and unbelievably she saw that Blanche was not alone!

"You whore! You harlot!" Mr. Bischoffsheim shouted at her.

Blanche sat upright in the bed and the man beside her raised himself on his elbow.

"You swore to me when I forgave you last time that you would never do this again," Mr. Bischoffsheim stormed. "You are nothing but a street-walker, a low class *poule.*"

Now Linetta could see the man lying beside Blanche.

It was impossible not to recognise his thin cadaverous face and his deep-set eyes.

It was Jacques Vossin!

"Dear Bisch, don't upset yourself."

Blanche was speaking in quite an ordinary unruffled tone.

"You promised me, you swore to me by everything you hold sacred, that you loved me and that I could trust you!" Mr. Bischoffsheim shouted. "Curse you for crucifying me – *curse you – curse you!*"

Then incredibly, so that Linetta could hardly believe that it was happening, he began to weep.

Tears rolled down his heavy cheeks and he was snuffling as he repeated over and over again,

"I trusted you, you – promised me! *Curse you!*"

Linetta, hardly aware of what she was doing, put the basket of flowers down on the floor arid turning ran from the room.

As she went, she could still hear Mr. Bischoffsheim's sobbing cries.

She reached her own room, pulled open the door and locked it behind her.

It was an instinctive gesture to shut herself in, to find solitude and some sort of escape from what was happening. Then she flung herself down on the bed and hid her face in the pillow.

She was trembling all over, her hands were clenched and for some time it was difficult for her to breathe.

Gradually the chaotic confusion of her thoughts sorted themselves out and she could think more sensibly about what she had seen and heard without wanting to scream or be sick,

She felt as if the picture of Blanche and Mr. Vossin lying side by side would be engraved on her mind for ever.

Blanche, a beautiful voluptuous pink-and-white Goddess, beside the sallow-skinned Mr. Vossin with the bones of his neck and his shoulders prominent and hairs on his bare chest.

Linetta had never seen a man naked and the fact that Mr. Vossin was unclothed was a shock in itself.

Now she could remember, although she had not taken it in at the time, that his clothes had been thrown untidily over a chair beside the bed, his shoes on the floor and his shirt gleaming white in the shadows.

'How *could* she? How could she let him touch her?' Linetta asked herself.

Then vividly and horrifyingly she realised that Blanche slept in her blue and white bed with Mr. Bischoffsheim.

Linetta was so innocent and so young that she had never really understood that men and women slept together and that they were naked.

The only people she had ever seen in bed had been her mother and Mademoiselle when she had been dying.

When she had thought of marriage, she had known that a husband and wife were close to each other, that they kissed and loved one another, but the full significance of their closeness had never been clearly defined or comprehended by her because she had never come face to face with it.

Now for the first time she considered what she had seen and in that moment she grew up.

Life was no longer a Fairytale, a fantasy or a stage where men and women romantically clothed acted out their lines but had no contact with reality.

It seemed to her now that ever since she came to Paris, Blanche had been acting a part, not only at the theatre but also in this rich, luxurious over-ornamented house that was paid for by Mr. Bischoffsheim.

He was Blanche's lover – Linetta faced the word. He was not a dear friend. He was her *lover*!

While Linetta still did not understand the full sense of what that meant, she knew now that it was something that involved getting into bed together naked!

It would only be possible to do such things with a man, she thought, if one loved him overwhelmingly so that nothing mattered except love.

But Blanche was surely not in love with Mr. Vossin and the mere fact that she could let him touch her showed that she was not in love with Mr. Bischoffsheim either.

In which case it was horrible and there seemed no point in it – until one remembered the big box of jewels locked away in the Boule writing desk.

Linetta lay for a long time going over and over in her mind what had happened, keeping her face hidden deep in the pillow for fear she might inadvertently hear, even behind the locked door of her bedroom, Mr. Bischoffsheim's sobs echoing down the passage.

It would in fact have been impossible because her room was too far away. But still she was afraid, still she shrank from further contact, from what she knew was horrible and unclean.

*

It was three hours later, and the stars were already fading from the sky, before finally Linetta rose to take off her gown and undress.

Although it was a warm night, she was shivering with cold and, when she finally climbed into bed, the blankets might have been made of paper. She was still trembling and it was impossible to sleep.

Now she understood so much that had puzzled her and so much that she had been unable to comprehend.

One thing she could understand and that was what Blanche had been trying to say to her earlier in the day when she showed her those jewels.

Mr. Vossin was rich. Had he not offered her everything he possessed?

Linetta thought, with a cynicism she had never felt before, that tomorrow Blanche would be able to add more diamonds, besides the necklace from Mr. Bischoffsheim, to her collection.

As the sun lit the darkness in her room, she rose from her bed and dressed herself.

She went to the wardrobe and, ignoring the beautiful gowns that were hanging there, took from the far corner where the maid had put them one of the gowns that she had brought with her from England.

It was a very plain blue muslin with little white cuffs and collar that she had sewn on to it herself.

She put it on and, having arranged her hair in the simple chignon that she had always worn at home, found the plain straw bonnet that she had travelled in. She put it on and tied the ribbons under her chin.

She opened the door of her bedroom, the house was very quiet and she doubted if even the servants were awake at this hour.

She went on tiptoe down the stairs, not looking at Blanche's door as she passed it, although aware that it was tightly closed.

What had happened after she had run away last night she had no idea about. She supposed that Mr. Vossin had left and perhaps Mr. Bischoffsheim had forgiven Blanche and stayed.

She felt as if she could still hear his ugly gulping sobs and somehow it was more degrading than when he had sworn at Blanche and cursed her.

Linetta let herself quietly out of the front door.

The sunshine was pale gold in the empty avenue and the trees with their blossoms in flower were silhouetted against the pale blue of the sky.

But for Linetta the darkness in her heart made her find no beauty anywhere.

She knew that she had to get away and think.

She felt that Blanche's house was stifling her, the very richness of it, the scented atmosphere and the fragrance of the hothouse flowers, all combined to muffle everything but a feeling of disgust.

She walked down the *Avenue de Friedland* and turned into the *Rue St. Honoré*.

She remembered that when they had been driving, Blanche had pointed out to her the British Embassy and she had noticed almost opposite it that there was a Church.

Vaguely Linetta thought it would be an Anglican Church. She was afraid of entering a Catholic one with its candles, its smell of incense and its lavish ornamentation, which would remind her of the opulence that she had seen everywhere else in Paris.

She longed for the plain whitewashed walls of the little Church at home where her mother's funeral service had been held.

She felt only in such surroundings could she find the help that she sought.

It was quite a long walk down the *Rue St. Honoré* and by the time she reached the British Embassy there were many more people in the street.

The linkmen were now snuffing the gaslights, the tradesmen were passing in their high-wheeled carts and there were a number of people soberly and poorly dressed obviously on their way to work.

Looking at them Linetta knew the answer to her own question before she reached the Church.

She had to find work!

She must do what she had intended to do when she first came to Paris – work to support herself.

She saw the Church ahead of her and, although she was half-afraid that it would be locked, when she pushed the heavy door it opened.

She went in.

It was an old Church, but it was, as she had hoped and expected, plain and unadorned. There were no images of Saints and no candles. There was nothing on the altar but a plain brass cross and it smelt of age and dust but nothing else.

Linetta knelt down in the first pew she came to and, as she bent her head to pray, she felt as if her mother was beside her.

It was a feeling that she had not had when her mother died, when she had cried out to her in the darkness of the night, feeling that it was impossible that she had gone and she would see her no more.

But now her mother was there, quite unmistakably beside her, comforting her, helping and sustaining her in a way that she had not known since she was a child.

"Help me, Mama," Linetta whispered. "Tell me what I am to do. I know now that what I intended was wrong and you would not have approved. But it seemed right because I – love him."

She paused and waited almost as if her mother would speak, but, although there was no answer, Linetta knew that she was not alone.

The hard taut feeling that had been in her chest all night was dissolving and she was no longer tense and no longer so afraid.

'How was I to know, Mama, that life is like that or that people could behave in such a way?' she asked.

She recognised as she spoke that the shock of what she had seen in Blanche's bedroom had almost paralysed her mind.

But now she was beginning to think and she knew quite clearly, as if her mother was speaking to her, that she could have nothing more to do with Blanche or the life that she led.

It was a world that she could take no part in and she knew that everything that had happened since she came to Paris must be erased as if it had been written on a slate that could be wiped pristine clean.

She must start again, start from the very beginning and start from the moment that she had left the *Gare du Nord* intending to work and make money by teaching.

For a long time Linetta knelt in the quietness of the Church.

Gradually it seemed to her, because her mother was beside her, the horror of what had happened was moving away and she could see it in its true perspective.

It might be Blanche's life, but it could never be hers!

It was not for her to judge whether Blanche was right or wrong in her behaviour.

She only knew that for her it would be degrading and therefore she could have no part in it.

It was perhaps an hour later that Linetta realised that her knees were aching from kneeling for so long and her whole body felt cramped.

She sat back in the pew and gazed at the coloured glass of the East window.

'Help me – please help me, God,' she prayed. 'I *must* find work.'

Then she rose to walk from the Church, feeling like a soldier going into battle. There were so many things she must do, but uppermost in her mind was the thought that she would have to tell the Marquis.

She must make him understand and make him realise that she could never live with him in the little house that they had chosen together and never belong to him as he wanted her to do.

'It was my fault,' Linetta told herself bravely. 'I forced myself upon him and I have no one to blame but myself for what has happened.'

At the same time she knew that even to think of what she must tell him made her heart beat quicker and she felt a fear rising within her so that her mouth became dry.

'He will understand,' she murmured to herself with a confidence that she did not really feel. "He *must* understand."

By now she had reached the back of the Church, when, as she turned to open the door, she saw a noticeboard.

An idea came to her.

Perhaps she could ask the Vicar if he knew of a school or a private family where she could teach.

She looked at the board and saw that there were notices giving the times of the Services on Sundays and weekdays.

There were others regarding meetings of Clubs.

And then she saw written on a card the words,

"Teacher in French and English wanted for a number of children of British residents in Paris aged between four and eight."

Linetta read it and re-read it.

This, she knew, was the answer to her prayer.

CHAPTER SEVEN

The Marquis arrived at the *Avenue de Friedland* at eleven o'clock. As the footman let him into the hall, he saw a large number of trunks that he guessed must belong to Linetta.

"M'mselle asks you to wait in the smoking room, my Lord," the footman said and led him into the room decorated in Oriental fashion where Linetta had been so surprised on her arrival to see cigarette holders.

He waited a few moments, gazing out of the window.

Then he heard Linetta come into the room and turned with a smile on his lips, which faded abruptly when he saw her.

It was not only the clothes she was wearing that told him that something was wrong but also the expression on her face.

"What has happened? Why are you dressed like that?" he enquired.

She walked slowly towards him and he saw that she was finding it hard to answer him.

"Something has upset you. What is it?" he demanded, as she did not speak.

"I have to – tell you," Linetta began in a very low voice, "that I – have found – employment and I therefore cannot come with you this morning – as you expected."

"Employment? What sort of employment?" the Marquis quizzed her sharply.

"They require a teacher for the children of some of the British residents in Paris. I have spoken with the Chaplain

~165~

of the British Embassy Church and he has – arranged it for – me."

Her voice was indistinct and she did not look at him as she spoke, her eyelashes dark against the unnatural pallor of her face.

"Whatever has happened, my darling?" the Marquis asked. "Why are you doing this? When I left you last night, you were so certain that we would be happy."

"I have – changed my mind. I cannot – explain why. You must only – believe me when I tell you that I – cannot do what we – planned."

There was a note in her voice that told the Marquis how much she was suffering.

"If something or somebody has upset you must tell me about it," he pleaded. "You know I will look after you and protect you from anything that is harmful or unpleasant."

"No," Linetta insisted, "no, you cannot do that!"

Her voice was unexpectedly firm and then, twisting her fingers together, she went on,

"I am only so ashamed and – distressed that you should have spent so much – money on my clothes. They are packed up and waiting for you in the hall. Perhaps you could – sell them or give them to – someone else."

"They were a present for you, Linetta."

"I would have no use – for them. And now I must go."

The Marquis, reached out his arms as if to put them around her, but she backed away from him.

"Please don't touch me," she urged him. "I love you – I shall always love you. But I know that what I am doing now is right and what we – intended to do was – wrong!"

"If you will tell me what has upset you," the Marquis said quietly, "we can talk it over together. Then I know it will not seem so frightening or disturbing because we will be sharing it."

"I want to – do – that," Linetta replied and he saw that her eyes were full of tears. "But there is really – nothing to talk about – nothing to say except – goodbye!"

Her voice broke on the words.

Then, as the Marquis stood looking at her at a loss as to what to say or do, she gave him a piteous little glance and turning round left the room.

He stood for a moment hardly able to take in the fact that she had left him and yet he sensed that she had meant what she said.

This was not the radiant happy girl who had lifted her face to his last night and who had said that she loved him.

This was a stranger, yet someone who despite her tears had a firmness and a resolution in her voice which told the Marquis that it would be difficult to make her change her mind.

Nevertheless he had no intention of losing Linetta and he told himself that the first thing he must do was to find out what had upset her.

*

The bedroom that Linetta was shown into in the *Rue d'Aguesseau*, where the British Embassy Church was situated, was small and dark and looked out onto a yard at the back.

When she had asked the Chaplain where she could stay, telling him that she had no knowledge of Paris, he had recommended a hostel where various female members of the Embassy staff were accommodated.

"It is kept by a Mrs. Matthews," he said. "She may be full, but I doubt it. Anyway tell her that I have sent you and ask her to do her very best to find you a room, at least until you have time to look round for yourself."

Mrs. Matthews was a grey-haired Scotswoman with a commanding personality, who made Linetta feel as if she was a delinquent schoolgirl.

"I cannot promise to keep you for more than two weeks, Miss Falaise," she said. "But at least temporarily you will have a roof over your head."

"Thank you very much," Linetta replied.

"I ask my boarders to be punctual for meals and no visitors are allowed in the bedrooms."

She said the last words almost fiercely, as if she fancied that Linetta might wish to entertain in the room, which was so small that there was hardly space to move.

"No, of course not," Linetta agreed.

"And everyone has to be in by ten o'clock at night except in special circumstances," Mrs. Matthews added.

When she had left, Linetta took off her bonnet, sat down on the bed and put her hands up to her face.

It was hard to think of the surprise and consternation on the Marquis's face when she had told him that she must leave him. Even now she could not realise that she had deliberately cut him out of her life and she would never see him again.

'I love him. *I love him*!' she told herself.

But she knew that, after what she had seen in Blanche's bedroom, she could not stay with him and could not make herself liable to the epithets that Mr. Bischoffsheim had shouted at Blanche.

'I love him,' Linetta told herself, 'but our love could not survive in such circumstances.'

She must have sat for a long time on her bed with her face in her hands. She was not crying, she was past everything but a kind of numb despair that seemed to paralyse not only her brain but also her heart.

Then there came a sharp rap at the door.

Linetta raised her head.

"There's a gentleman downstairs to see you, miss," a woman's voice said in English, "and Mrs. Matthews says he's not to stay long as luncheon will be ready in ten minutes."

Linetta knew at once who was downstairs and her first impulse was to say that she would not see the Marquis.

Then she had the feeling that he would insist and it would be better for her to tell him personally that he must go away rather than send messages through servants.

She rose to her feet and, without even glancing in the mirror to see if her hair was tidy, she walked slowly down the stairs.

There was a sitting room on the right of the front door where Mrs. Matthews had interviewed her when she had first arrived.

She found the Marquis standing in the middle of it looking very tall, distinguished and broad-shouldered against the shabby beige-coloured curtains and the cheap uncomfortable furniture, which was mostly covered in horsehair.

She closed the door behind her.

Then, as she turned to look at him, their eyes met and it was impossible to move.

He walked towards her and taking her hand lifted it to his lips.

"Why did you not tell me, my darling, what had happened?" he asked.

Linetta gave an inarticulate little murmur and turned her head away from him.

"I do understand how much it must have upset you," he said. "It was all my fault for leaving you in that house and for allowing you to consort with such people."

"No, it was not – your fault," Linetta said, finding her voice as if with an effort. "It was mine. I knew it was – wrong from the very beginning, but it seemed so – fascinating and – so glamorous and it is only now that I realise that it was all an illusion."

She drew in her breath and went on as if she was forced to do so,

"It is like the theatre which looks gay and – exciting at night, but dingy, dirty and – sordid when the lights are not – lit."

The Marquis again raised Linetta's hand to his lips.

She quivered at the touch of his mouth, but she went on bravely,

"It is an illusion like the beauty and extravagance of the Paris one sees in the *Bois de Boulogne* and in the new boulevards, but behind them there is squalor and children dying of starvation."

There was a little throb in her voice and then she looked up at him and continued,

"It was an illusion too when we believed – that we could be happy. It sounded so plausible that I should be a 'second wife', your *chère amie*, but what I would have been in – reality was the – vulgar names that Mr. Bischoffsheim called – Blanche."

The last words were almost incoherent and tears ran down Linetta's cheeks.

"Our love is not an illusion, Linetta," the Marquis asserted in his deep voice. "I love you and I want you for my wife."

He felt her stiffen and for a moment her fingers tightened on his.

"Will you marry me, my darling?"

"No – I cannot! Please you must not – ask me."

"Why not?" the Marquis enquired. "You must not be angry with me, although indeed you should be, for not realising that what we planned together was not really what either of us wanted. We belong to each other, you are mine, Linetta! It was only that everything happened so quickly and I was such a fool that I did not fully understand that I did not want you as my mistress but as my wife."

Linetta. took her hands from his.

"It's – impossible!"

"Why?" the Marquis asked. "Why should you say that?"

"Because I am well aware of your – importance in England. Just as in France the marriages of Noblemen like yourself are arranged with – a woman who is your social equal – a woman who will bring you something in exchange for the position – you give her."

"Do you really think that is the sort of marriage I want?" the Marquis asked with a smile on his lips. "If it had been, Linetta, I would have been married long ago. But I have remained a bachelor simply because I have never fallen in I love."

He paused and added,

"Not until I met you, my precious."

Linetta walked away from him to stand gazing out of the window onto the road.

"I want to marry you. As I love you – that is what I have – longed for in my heart – but I have always – known it is impossible – quite – quite impossible!"

"Why?" the Marquis demanded.

"For one reason," she replied, "I don't even know the name of my father."

The Marquis moved nearer to her.

"How is that possible? Do you mean to – say that Falaise is your mother's name?"

Linetta nodded.

"I thought it was strange, when you said that your father was English, that he should have a French name, but I was not particularly interested in your parents, only in you."

"You cannot marry anyone without a name, without relations and with no – background."

The Marquis did not speak and after a moment she carried on,

"Even to think that we might be married in such circumstances is just another – illusion."

She turned her head again to look out of the window and he saw that she was crying.

"There must be an answer to this problem," the Marquis said after a moment. "You told me the reason for you coming to Paris was that your Governess had died and since your mother's death you had lived on her savings."

"Yes – that is what I – told you," Linetta agreed.

"I think you said too that until your mother died she had an allowance which came from your father's Executors."

"No, it came from a Bank in Oxford. It was delivered by a clerk every quarter day."

"And he told you after your mother's death that there would be no more money?" the Marquis questioned.

"We received this," Linetta replied.

She had brought her handbag with her when she came downstairs as it contained all the money she possessed. In it as well were her passport and the letter that Mademoiselle had told her to take from the desk.

Linetta had read it so often that she knew it by heart.

Inscribed in a clerk's hand were the words,

> *"In consequence of the death of Mrs. Yvonne Falaise this is to inform you that the monies paid to her every quarter day will cease forthwith from this, the twenty-fifth day of September in the year of Our Lord 1867.*
> *Yours respectfully,*
> *Herman Clegg,*
> *Secretary."*

That was all.

Linetta opened the letter, which had become creased from being carried in her handbag and passed it to the Marquis.

He took it from her automatically, his eyes on her face, his expression almost as worried and anxious as hers.

Then, as if he could find no words to articulate what was in his thoughts, he looked down at the letter.

Suddenly he became rigid.

There was something in his stillness that frightened Linetta and, as he did not speak, she asked after a moment,

"What – is it?"

For a moment it seemed as if the Marquis was unable to answer her and then he said sharply in a voice that she had never heard from him before,

"Put on your travelling clothes and ask the servants to bring your luggage downstairs."

"What do you – mean?" Linetta asked. "What is it? Where do you – want me to go?"

"I am taking you back to England," the Marquis replied. "We are going to find out the truth about your father."

*

It seemed to Linetta when they reached England the following day that it had been a journey that she had been caught up in in an oppressive nightmare that she could not awake from.

When the Marquis had told her they were going to England she could not understand that he really meant that he was taking her there and that he had suddenly become a different person from the man who had been pleading with her to marry him.

"Does the letter tell you how I can find out – about my father?" she asked when, because the Marquis would not listen to her protests, she found herself driving through the streets with him towards the *Gare du Nord*.

"Yes," he replied, "but I do *not* wish to discuss it with you yet."

"You think you really can find out – who my father was?" Linetta insisted.

"When I know the truth, you shall hear it too," the Marquis answered. "Until then there is nothing to gain by guessing or inventing what we cannot substantiate."

Linetta realised that in some way the letter had upset him. Yet there seemed to be little to learn from the few sentences that she herself had read over and over again.

Then, as she puzzled over the Marquis's attitude, she remembered that the letter was written on writing paper, which was engraved with an address.

It had meant nothing to her when she had taken it from the desk and she was sure that it meant nothing to Mademoiselle.

The Castle,
Canterbury,
Kent.

.But she knew now that what had seemed to her to be of no importance was of definite significance to the Marquis, but because of his strange manner she found it impossible to question him further.

Because he had ordered her to do so, she put on her travelling gown with its dark cape that she had worn when they had first met and hastily packed the gown that she was wearing in a small, worn leather trunk that had been carried up to her room.

The footman had then taken it downstairs.

When the Marquis had joined her in the hall and they went outside, Linetta saw not only that the Duke's carriage was awaiting them but also a *voiture,* which was piled high with the trunks that she had left behind in the *Avenue de Friedland.* She glanced at them but said nothing.

Then the Marquis had ordered the coachman to drive to the *Gare du Nord* and told the footman to order the *cocher* to follow them.

He had spoken to Mrs. Matthews while Linetta was upstairs, because when she joined him and said hesitatingly,

"I think I must – tell the Chaplain of the Church that I am – going away."

"I have already asked Mrs. Matthews to inform him that you have to return to England on urgent family business."

The Marquis spoke in a manner that made Linetta look at him wonderingly.

There was a darkness in his expression and a frown between his eyes that she could not understand.

What did he know?

Why had he changed?

She was to ask herself the same question over and over again as they travelled by train to Calais where they arrived very late at night, or rather early in the morning, to stay in a somewhat uncomfortable hotel on the seafront.

Linetta was so tired, having been awake the night before, that she slept for a little while in the train and fell asleep in the hotel as soon as her head touched the pillow.

But when she joined the Marquis at breakfast downstairs the next morning, she had the feeling that he had passed a sleepless night.

There were dark lines under his eyes and she realised that, while he talked to her with his usual courtesy, he did not look at her and she recognised too that he was deliberately avoiding anything that might make their conversation intimate.

He engaged a private cabin on the Steamer, but, although it was rather windy and the sea was sometimes rough, he spent the whole voyage walking around the deck.

Linetta sat alone trying not to remember how kind he had been when she sought his protection from the man who had frightened her on the journey from England to France.

Now that she was returning to England she kept wondering why the Marquis had brought her back, especially as he seemed to wish to have no further contact with her.

And yet, Linetta told herself despairingly, she loved him more than ever!

She had only to look at him to feel that her love was an agonising pain in her breast and she had only to hear him speak to feel a little tremor run through her.

The rapture, the ecstasy and the wonder she had felt when he had first kissed her in the *Bois de Boulogne*, when she had known that they belonged to each other, had gone.

Instead there was only the misery of knowing that there was a barrier between them that she did not understand as well as a gulf between their stations in life that could never be bridged.

'I love him! *I love him!*' she told herself and wondered why, when now she could mean nothing in his life, he was taking all the trouble to find out about her father.

Alone in the cabin, which smelt of oil from the engines, the salt and the sea, she had a horrifying thought that perhaps her father had been a criminal.

Supposing he had done something really wrong and the Marquis was taking her home to make reparation for his crimes?

Then she told herself firmly that she was just being imaginative.

Her mother had always spoken of her father as a wonderful person and she would never have mourned anyone who had not lived up to her own standards and ideals of what was right and what was wrong.

Yet if her father had been all that she had imagined him to be when she was a child, if he had been the hero that she had enshrined in her imagination, why then did the Marquis look so grim?

Why did he no longer speak of their love or ask her again to marry him as he had done in the hostel?

It was all too fantastic a puzzle for her to unravel.

She only knew that she felt depressed to the point when it was hard to control her tears and the pain in her chest seemed to increase every time the Marquis came near her.

They arrived at Dover to find that it was raining and the sky overcast and Linetta thought that the sunshine and beauty of Paris had been left behind for ever.

Again she told herself severely that it had been only part of the illusion that could no longer mean anything in her life.

She had to face reality, as she had been trying to do when the Marquis had taken her away from the post she had found herself and brought her back to England.

'Please God, don't let us find out anything horrible or wrong about Papa,' she whispered beneath her breath. 'Please let him be noble, fine and upright as I have always believed him to be.'

Again they were in a fast train, travelling through the countryside at a very much quicker speed than the stagecoach that Linetta had travelled to Dover in.

She had ceased to talk to the Marquis or make any effort to exchange anything but commonplaces about where she should sit or whether she would like anything to eat or drink.

Whenever she looked at him, she saw that his mouth was set in a hard line and his chin seemed very square.

They were alone in the carriage and she had an insane desire to fling herself into his arms, to beg him to hold her close and tell her that he still loved her.

'What does anything matter but our love?' she so wanted to say.

Despairingly she thought that she had thrown away all the happiness that she would ever know in her life for a misery and loneliness that would be hers for the rest of her existence.

'Why was I so stupid?' she asked herself. 'Why did I not accept what was offered to me and be content?'

Then she recalled how close her mother had seemed to her in the Church and she had known that any happiness she found with the Marquis in the little house near the

Champs-Élysées would not have been real but only a *golden illusion.*

*

It was about the middle of the afternoon that the Marquis drew his gold watch from his waistcoat pocket and announced,

"We shall arrive in ten minutes."

"Where?" Linetta asked.

"Canterbury," he replied.

Linetta looked at him in surprise until she remembered the address on the top of the letter.

Now she understood where they were going, to The Castle, to find Mr. Herman Clegg, because, having written the letter, he must have some knowledge of her father.

A hundred questions came to her lips, but because the Marquis seemed detached and distant she said nothing, but only watched him with an expression of helplessness that made her look very young and very pathetic.

They stepped out of the train at Canterbury Station and, when she saw that there were a number of his servants waiting for them, she knew why the Marquis had sent a telegram before they boarded the train at Dover.

"Good afternoon, my Lord. It's very nice to see you back."

"You have brought a landau for the luggage?"

"Yes, my Lord, the carriage is this way."

They were shown into a comfortable closed carriage drawn by a team of four superlative horses in which they drove away from the Station at what seemed to Linetta to be a fantastically fast pace.

The Marquis sat in a corner of the carriage and seemed intent on watching the countryside that they were passing through.

After they had driven for a mile or so, Linetta asked him in a low voice,

"Where are we – going?"

"To my home."

"You live near Canterbury?"

"Yes."

She thought this over and knew that it was why the Marquis's attitude had altered when he had seen the address on the letter.

She longed to ask more questions, but because she loved him she sensed that he was not only tense but was determined not to gratify her curiosity.

'What is the secret about Papa?' she asked herself despairingly again and again and finding no answer lapsed into silence.

After driving for three-quarters of an hour, suddenly they turned in through two lodge gates and were driving down a long avenue of oak trees.

It was difficult to see ahead until suddenly the avenue turned and in front of them Linetta saw a large, magnificent grey stone building.

She looked at it and then saw unmistakably that it was a Castle.

It was very awe-inspiring and she was just about to ask the Marquis frankly if this was The Castle that Mr. Clegg had written the letter from, when he said in the same cold detached voice that he had used to her on the whole journey,

"I want you to wait for me, Linetta, in the carriage. I have some enquiries to make inside The Castle. When I have done so, I will join you and I hope be able to explain many of the issues that perplex you."

"I will – wait," Linetta responded in a low voice.

The carriage drew up outside a long flight of wide steps and servants ran down to open the door as the Marquis stepped out.

Then he must have given instructions to the coachman because the carriage moved away from the door along the big gravel sweep that encircled The Castle.

It stopped on the other side so that Linetta looked out at a lake that lay below and at the gardens sloping down to it.

She let down the window and felt the warm soft spring air against her cheeks. It felt very fresh and spring-like and slowly she drew in a deep breath, hoping that perhaps it would calm her feeling of agitation.

The Marquis walked into the marble hall automatically handing his hat, gloves and travelling cape to the butler.

"Nice to see you back, my Lord, we weren't expecting you to return so quickly."

"I am aware of that," the Marquis replied. "Where is Mr. Clegg?"

"I expect he's in the estate office, my Lord. Shall I tell him you wish to see him?"

"No," the Marquis replied, "I will find him for myself."

He walked away and the butler looked after him in perplexity.

It was most unlike the Marquis to speak in such a harsh voice and not to enquire about the wellbeing of The Castle and the staff in his absence.

The Marquis moved down the broad corridor to where at the far end there was the estate office containing plans and maps of the estate and where Mr. Herman Clegg, who acted as his private secretary, had his desk.

He was an elderly man and had been in the service of the Marquis's father. The smooth running of The Castle and all the other family properties rested entirely upon his shoulders.

When the Marquis entered the office, it was to find Herman Clegg giving instructions to a junior clerk who, clutching his papers, immediately disappeared into an adjoining room.

"This is a surprise, my Lord," Mr. Clegg exclaimed. "We expected you to be away for several more months."

"That is what I expected myself," the Marquis replied, "but I came back to ask you for an explanation of this."

As he spoke, he put the letter that Linetta had given him down on the desk.

Mr. Clegg looked at it.

"It is signed with your name," the Marquis pointed out as he did not speak. "I want you to tell me why it was written and on whose instructions."

"On the instructions of her Ladyship, my Lord. She dictated it to me and I merely sent it to a Bank in Oxford, asking them to convey the information to the person or persons concerned."

"Is that all you know?"

"That's all, my Lord."

The Marquis picked up the letter.

"Will I find her Ladyship at the Dower House?"

"As a matter of fact, my Lord, she is in The Castle at this moment. She called to see Mrs. Briggs, the housekeeper, who, as hour Lordship knows, has not been in good health. She arrived about an hour ago and should in fact still be with Mrs. Briggs."

"Ask her Ladyship to come to the White Drawing Room immediately," the Marquis then said.

"Very good, my Lord."

The Marquis turned and walked out of the estate office.

As he went towards the White Drawing Room, he thought it was typical that his stepmother should be in The Castle.

He had made it clear after he inherited that he would not have her interfering or, as he put it to himself, snooping round The Castle and making trouble.

She had always been a tiresome domineering woman with whom he had little in common and whom ever since he had been a small boy he had disliked seeing in his mother's place.

He did not have to wait long in the White Drawing Room before the Dowager Marchioness came sweeping into the room, her black silk bustle rustling behind her. The long strings of pearls she wore found the ample proportions of her bosom an effective background for their translucent sheen.

Although the Dowager Marchioness had a cold hard manner, she had been extremely good-looking in her youth.

The Marquis had never admired her, but she had been painted by a number of artists and there was no doubt that, wearing the Darleston jewellery, she stood out in any ballroom.

"This is certainly an unexpected return, Salvin!" she exclaimed to her stepson. "I understood that you would be away for the whole summer."

"I returned because I deemed it imperative for me to have an explanation regarding this letter, which was shown to me whilst I was in Paris."

The Marquis held out Linetta's letter as he spoke and, although the Dowager Marchioness took it from him, there was some delay before she opened her lorgnettes, which was hanging from a chain round her neck and had somehow become entangled with her pearls.

Finally she raised the glasses to her high-bridged nose and read the letter through without speaking.

Then she said,

"It's a matter that need not concern you, Salvin."

"As it happens, it is very much my concern," the Marquis replied. "I understand that you instructed Clegg to stop the monies that I gather my father had paid to a Mrs. Falaise for some years. Why?"

"The woman was dead."

"Did you not know that she had a child?"

"Yes, I knew that."

The Marquis drew in his breath.

"Is she my sister?"

His voice as he spoke seemed to be half-strangled in his throat.

Although the Dowager Marchioness was not aware of it, his hands were clenched until the knuckles showed white.

There was a pause.

"No, she is not your sister," the Dowager Marchioness replied.

"How do you know? Was this Mrs. Falaise one of father's lady – friends?"

There was a perceptible pause between the last two words.

"She was not!" the Dowager Marchioness said firmly. "Although, as you well know, there were plenty of others."

The Marquis relaxed.

The darkness that had been there ever since he left Paris vanished from his face.

He walked across to the open window as if in sudden need of fresh air.

The Dowager Marchioness's eyes followed him with an expression of astonishment as she seated herself on the sofa.

"Why are you so interested, Salvin?"

"I should like you to tell me all about this Mrs. Falaise and why my father was sending her money every quarter day."

"It's a story that the fewer people who know about it the better!" the Dowager Marchioness replied. "But as unfortunately, by some means I cannot guess, you have come into possession of this letter, I had better tell you the facts."

"I want them all and the truth," the Marquis asserted firmly.

"I don't know whether you remember your father talking about a distant cousin called 'Rupert Darle'?" the Dowager began.

"I think I remember him," the Marquis said doubtfully. "He was much older than me and I believe I am right in saying that he died rather tragically."

"This is right," the Dowager Marchioness agreed.

"I remember hearing about it, although I was a child at the time," the Marquis said. "In what way is he connected with this letter?"

"Your father was always very fond of Rupert. He hated his own father bitterly and so, whenever he was in trouble, he always asked for your father's help and he was never refused."

"Go on," the Marquis prompted.

"He got into all sorts of difficulties when he was at Eton and would have been sacked had it not been for your father's intervention. It was always your father who had to cope with his wild behaviour, never his own family."

The Dowager Marchioness paused and then she went on,

"When Rupert went up to Oxford University, he immediately fell in love with the daughter of one of the Dons. She was French."

The Marquis seated himself beside his stepmother on the sofa. There was no doubt that he was listening intently to every word she said.

"Although no one had any idea of it, Rupert married her! It was, of course, a secret marriage except that, since she was so in love with him, her father gave his consent."

The Dowager Marchioness made a little gesture with her hands.

"It was a mad idea, absolutely mad! The girl was seventeen and Rupert was nineteen. All the time he was supposed to be studying they were living together and from what Rupert told your father afterwards they were extremely happy."

"There is no doubt as to the validity of the marriage?" the Marquis enquired.

"None at all," his stepmother replied. "The Marriage Certificate is somewhere amongst your father's private papers."

"Please continue," the Marquis urged her.

"When it was time for Rupert to leave Oxford University, his father insisted that he should go round the world. Rupert made every possible objection, but Stephen Darle was a very dominating man. He threatened to disinherit Rupert if he did not obey him."

The Dowager paused before she went on,

"Before he left Rupert came to see your father and told him about his marriage. Your father was shocked by the secrecy of it.

"'You must tell your father,' he told Rupert.

"'If I do, he will cut me off without a penny.'

"'Then what do you intend to do?'

"'Make my fortune while I am away!'

"Your father thought it unlikely as Rupert was going abroad with a pocketbook full of introductions to Royalty, Prime Ministers and social celebrities! People who are not likely to provide business contacts."

The Dowager paused to add sourly,

"But, of course, your father's good nature made him promise to keep Rupert's secret and provide for his wife while he was abroad."

"What happened then?" the Marquis asked impatiently.

"While Rupert was away, his father arranged a marriage for him with the Duke of Harpenden's daughter."

The Marquis made an exclamation of astonishment, but he did not interrupt.

"They had known each other for some time," his stepmother went on, "and I suppose the girl found him very attractive, which indeed he was."

"But surely Rupert had to tell her and his father the truth?"

'The engagement was announced without his expecting it at the party that was given to celebrate his return."

"What did he do then?" the Marquis asked.

"He came to see your father the next day," the Dowager replied. "He told him that Stephen, his father, was very ill. In fact the doctor had told him as soon as he set foot in the house that his heart was in such a bad state that a shock or anything that upset him would kill him."

The Dowager's lips tightened.

"Your father and I never cared for Stephen Darle, he was a man of ungovernable rages."

"What happened?"

"Rupert claimed that he was certain that his father would not live long and all he could do was to play for time. To produce a wife at this moment would, he was quite sure, precipitate his father's death."

"I do see it was a problem," the Marquis said reflectively. "What made it worse was that Stephen in his usual autocratic manner had sent a notice of the engagement to *The Gazette* without consulting his son."

"Had Rupert's wife nothing to say?" the Marquis enquired angrily.

"Rupert told your father that she was prepared to wait until Stephen was dead. Anyway she remained in obscurity as she had been when Rupert went abroad. Naturally she had to be provided for and Rupert had returned without a penny in his pocket. You can guess who paid it."

"My father!" the Marquis exclaimed automatically.

"Of course," she agreed. "Did your father ever refuse to help a lame dog or an impecunious relation?"

The Marquis did not reply and his stepmother continued,

"Rupert was drowned when saving his fiancée's life when their boat capsized during a boating party on the Thames."

"Good Lord!" the Marquis expostulated. "I had no idea that was what happened."

"It was a tragedy that never should have occurred," the Dowager said sternly, "and it put your father in a very difficult position."

"Why, when Rupert was dead, did he not reveal that he was married?" the Marquis asked her.

"He intended to do so, but, while the shock of Rupert's death did not kill Stephen, his life hung on a thread. Also Rupert was proclaimed a hero by the newspapers and his fiancée was broken-hearted."

"I can see the difficulty," the Marquis admitted slowly. "The Duke kept saying publicly how proud he would have been of his son-in-law and the girl fainted at his funeral. The Queen sent a telegram of condolence."

"So my father said nothing."

"He merely went on paying an allowance to Rupert's wife. It was doubtful whether, if the family had learnt of her existence, they would have accepted her under the circumstances. And the scandal would have affected us all."

"But morally it was inexcusable for her to be treated in such a disgraceful manner," the Marquis pointed out, "and, when she died, you told the Bank to terminate the allowance my father had made her."

The Dowager Marchioness rose to her feet.

"I saw no reason," she said in a cold voice, "why your father's estate should go on being bled to cover up Rupert's misalliance."

"Even though there was a child of the marriage?"

The Dowager Marchioness hesitated a moment.

"The Bank informed me that she existed when I stopped the payments, which had been made to her mother. Your father did not know about it and I don't think that Rupert had any idea that he had fathered a child. I can only imagine, if it was his, that his wife did not try to assert herself by insisting that he acknowledge it."

The Marquis rose to his feet and commented,

"She loved him enough to do what was best for him in his lifetime and for his memory when he was dead. In fact she loved him as few men are privileged to be loved."

His stepmother looked at him for a moment in perplexity.

Then she said sharply,

"This unsavoury business is best forgotten. Rupert is dead and his wife is dead too. The marriage is something that will never be known by anyone who might write the history of the family and I hope that you, Salvin, will never mention the subject again."

The Marquis gave a laugh of genuine amusement.

"That is something I am afraid will prove quite impossible!"

"But why?" his stepmother questioned.

"Because," he answered, "as it happens I am going to marry Cousin Rupert's daughter!"

He walked out of the White Drawing Room as he spoke leaving the Dowager Marchioness staring after him, her mouth open in amazement.

*

The Marquis hurried across the hall.

Outside he saw the carriage waiting on the gravel sweep and, when he reached it, the footman informed him,

"The young lady walked down to the lake, my Lord. I thought there was no harm in allowing her to do so."

"None at all," the Marquis replied. "You can send the carriage away, we shall not need it any more today."

"Very good, my Lord."

The footman climbed up onto the box as the carriage drove towards the stables and the Marquis walked over the green lawns.

The afternoon sun had come out to drive away the clouds and the sky was blue. It was reflected in the lake and the kingcups were splendidly golden along its banks.

The Marquis walked on, but there was no sign of Linetta. At the bottom of the bank there was a cluster of almond trees already in bloom.

Then at last he saw her under the trees, the rays of the sun glinting on her hair.

She had taken off her bonnet and was holding it by its ribbons and even in her plain unfashionable gown she portrayed a grace the Marquis had found in no other woman.

It made her look fragile and insubstantial as if she was a nymph who had strayed from the water of the lake to find the perfect background for her beauty against the pink-and-white blossom.

He drew a little nearer and she turned and then she saw him.

There was a sudden irrepressible gladness in her eyes before almost deliberately she swept it away with an expression of anxiety and apprehension.

The Marquis stood still in front of her, but he was smiling.

Then, as if the sunshine, the beauty of the blossom and their own feelings made them forget everything that had kept them apart, he held out his arms and Linetta ran into them.

She thought that it was like reaching Heaven to be close to him again and to know that he loved her and to feel that for one moment at least that she need no longer worry and no longer fight against him.

"Oh, my darling, my sweet! My precious little love!" the Marquis said unsteadily. "I love you, God, how I love you! And I thought I had lost you."

As if she could not help herself, Linetta raised her face to his and his lips were on hers, kissing her wildly, passionately and frantically until she could no longer think but only feel that she was a part of him.

"I love you!" he breathed. "And, darling, now we can be married! There is nothing to stop us – *nothing*!"

"B-but – Papa – " she stammered.

"You are my cousin, my sweet. Your father bore my family name of Darle and was a fourth or fifth cousin of mine, I cannot remember which!"

"Your cousin?" Linetta asked in a wondering tone.

"My cousin," the Marquis said firmly as if he would confirm it to himself.

She would never know, he thought, the agonies he had suffered when he had been afraid of a much nearer relationship.

"What was he like?" Linetta asked.

"He was tall and they tell me very good-looking," the Marquis replied. "He also had a charm that made everyone love him."

"Oh, I knew it. I knew it," Linetta interposed. "When I first saw you at Dover, I had a feeling that you were exactly what my Papa would have looked like if I had ever seen him. I must have known instinctively that you were related."

"Not too closely, but your real name is 'Linetta Darle' and, darling, apart from me you are no longer alone. You have quite a number of relations, we are a big family."

Linetta drew a little closer to him.

"I don't want a lot of relations," she affirmed. "I only want *you*."

"As I want you," the Marquis smiled. "We are going to be married immediately, my precious one, and we are going on our honeymoon, not to Paris, but to Venice, Italy, Greece anywhere you like as long as we can be together."

Linetta drew in her breath.

"Are you really – telling me – this? Is it true – really true that you will not be – ashamed of me, that I can marry you without feeling that I am – harming you in any way?"

"You loved me enough to refuse me," the Marquis said in his deep voice and there was a reverence in the way he spoke.

Linetta must never realise how weakly her father had behaved, he thought. It was so long ago that most people would have forgotten his engagement and those who had not could be persuaded to keep silent.

It would not be easy, but he would contrive it. On one point he was quite determined that Linetta would not meet her new relatives until they had been married for some time and she had grown used to the idea of being his wife.

He pulled her closer as he said,

"We are going to be married tomorrow or the next day by Special Licence. Then we are going to spend many, many months, my darling, getting to know each other."

He kissed her cheek, his lips lingering against the perfection of her skin before he went on,

"Have you forgotten that I have to show you how much I love you and teach you about love?"

'That would be more – wonderful than anything I can – imagine," Linetta whispered, "to be with you and to be – alone."

"There will be nobody else with us," the Marquis promised, "not until you have begun to be bored with me."

He saw the sudden question in her eyes and gave a little laugh as he added,

"I know I am repeating what you said to me, but I shall never be bored with you. You are everything I have ever longed for, everything that I ever wanted to find and indeed very nearly lost."

His lips found hers again as if he was reassuring himself that she was really there.

He kissed her at first gently and then passionately.

As she clung to him, vibrating to new sensations and new feelings that she had never known before, she found that the pain in her heart had gone.

She felt as though she could fly in the air and dance on the water.

"I love you! *I love you*!" she breathed.

"And I love you, my beautiful innocent darling."

She looked up at him and saw his dark handsome head silhouetted against the almond blossom on the trees.

"It is all so beautiful and so like a Fairy story," she whispered. "Are you quite certain it is not an illusion?"

"It is the truth, it is real, it is fact," he replied. "I love you and worship you. You have captured my heart, Linetta, and my whole future happiness lies in your hands."

Her eyes seemed to hold glorious sunshine and she laid her face against his shoulder.

"I will make you happy," she vowed, "I will love you – now and forever – with all my heart and soul."

'That is all I ask of life," the Marquis replied softly, "that you should love me as I love you."

His lips were on hers again and the only movement in their enchanted world was the petals of the almond blossoms falling gracefully around them.

This was no illusion, this was Heaven.

OTHER BOOKS IN THIS SERIES

The Barbara Cartland Eternal Collection is the unique opportunity to collect all five hundred of the timeless beautiful romantic novels written by the world's most celebrated and enduring romantic author.

Named the Eternal Collection because Barbara's inspiring stories of pure love, just the same as love itself, the books will be published on the internet at the rate of four titles per month until all five hundred are available.

The Eternal Collection, classic pure romance available worldwide for all time.